Vs.

THE BOOKIES

By the same author:

Baxter Vs. The Bookies — Published 2004
ISBN 09548 604 03

BAXTER

Vs.

THE BOOKIES

RACING STORIES

by

ROY GRANVILLE

Illustrations by LEZZ

Published by
Hayes Press
PO Box 489
Hayes
UB3 2WZ

First published in Great Britain in 2007 by

Hayes Press

PO Box 489

Hayes

UB3 2WZ

A CIP catalogue number is available from the British Library.

ISBN 978-0-9548604-1-7

Typeset by Tim Harris at www.theboxroom.com

Printed and bound in Great Britain by CPD, Wales.

At least 60% of horses don't really want to do their best. Winning doesn't mean all that much to them.

Lester Piggott

"Now that's what I call a piece of training!"

CONTENTS

CUTTING COSTS

Baxter was a racehorse tipster. However, the length of his greying hair suggested more a musician or hermit. He therefore presented himself at Arthur's Hairdressing Salon in Shepherd's Bush, which had been by appointment to Baxter for many years. A racing buff and punter, Arthur Thomas at least made the tiresome but necessary event tolerable.

Baxter wandered in, still absorbed in the Racing Post's form pages for Wolverhampton. He sat down on the bench, which registered unusually comfortable in his sub-conscious, and waited.

"Have you an appointment, sir?"

The voice sounded odd to Baxter who looked up at a brightly dressed young man who was regarding him with the eyes of a woman.

"Appointment?" frowned Baxter. "No, I haven't."

"No problem, I can still fit you in. This way please!"

The tall slim figure led Baxter towards a chair. Baxter was looking around. The bench hadn't been a bench but a sofa, there were large potted plants dotted about, yellow and chrome-fitted walls, diamond-shaped mirrors and, worst of all, there were two girls cutting men's hair. It didn't look like Arthur's, it didn't smell like Arthur's and yet it should have been Arthur's.

"Where's Arthur?" asked Baxter

"Mr Thomas is not here now, sir." The man had put a

green gown swiftly round Baxter's neck and pushed his head forward into a sink. "My name's Roger, I had the place re-fitted. D'you like it?"

Water was spraying onto Baxter's head.

"What d'you think you're doing?" he spluttered.

"Washing your hair, sir" said Roger condescendingly.

"But it isn't dirty" protested Baxter.

"We do it automatically, sir. It makes the hair nicer to cut."

"What's Arthur doing now?" asked Baxter, his words punctuated by the brisk rubbing of a towel around his head.

"Retired I believe. Did you know he won a million pounds on the pools?"

Baxter obviously didn't.

"Wow! One thousand big ones! And I was here only a couple of months ago."

"Yes, you shouldn't let your hair get so long next time" scolded Roger. He picked up a comb. "Now what style would you like?"

"Style?" queried Baxter. "I just want it cut."

"Any particular way, sir?" persisted Roger.

"Look!" Baxter held a strand of hair between his fingers "I've got these nearly all over - cut the ends off and put them back as they were."

Roger looked hurt, bounced his eyes and wielded his scissors in silence. Baxter didn't like the shop and Roger made him feel uncomfortable but he decided to make a charitable effort.

"D'you like racing?" he said without much hope.

"Racing?" said Roger. "What sort of racing?"

Baxter wished he hadn't asked.

"Pushed his head forward into a sink"

"Horseracing" he said.

The reply was indignant.

"My goodness, no! How dreadfully boring! Most sport is, I'm afraid."

Baxter put a mental line through Roger and endured the novelty of having his hair blow-dried. At home he'd have used the electric fire.

After paying an exorbitant £9.95, Baxter concluded that Roger wouldn't need to win the pools to retire. However, the news of Arthur's good fortune, pre-occupied Baxter all the way home. He had never understood people doing the football pools as it seemed you had as much chance of winning as finding a travel agency on Alcatraz. He wondered if he should now devote some time to the game before realising that the only footballer he'd ever heard of was Stanley Matthews.

Shortly after his haircut with Roger, Baxter was at Windsor for an evening meeting. The first race was a big field of three-year-old maidens and he'd already decided it was not a race to bet on. He was leaning on the parade ring rail when he noticed a natty line in racing silks. The jockey appeared to be wearing graph paper on which crosses had been marked.

Baxter looked at his race card for the description – 'White, blue vertical and horizontal lines with eight blue crosses, white cap with eight blue crosses'. Above was the owner's name, Mr A.Thomas and the horse was named Jackpot.

It just had to be Arthur felt Baxter and pushed his way across to the far side of the ring where the jockey was now standing in the middle of a small group. Baxter recognised Arthur, a small dapper man with a grey moustache and ears like a giraffe.

The bell went and the jockeys started to get on.

"Arthur!" shouted Baxter as the group moved off.

The little man beamed as he recognised Baxter. He came across and offered his hand.

"How are you?" he said.

"Well, not as well as you" smiled Baxter. "What about your horse, should I back it?"

"No" whispered Arthur "just watch it this time." He looked back anxiously to the group. "Look, I'm with some friends now but I'm going over to Finnie's stables tomorrow. Give me a ring if you want to come - it'll probably be worth your while." He handed Baxter a card.

Jackpot came seventh in the race, making late headway after being dropped out early on. Baxter put down his binoculars and had the distinct impression there was a race to be won with the horse.

The rest of the card looked difficult and surprisingly none of Baxter's acquaintances knew anything of use. The only horse he may have backed was terrible value at odds-on and its subsequent defeat was down to the jockey getting himself so boxed in that Baxter immediately diagnosed agoraphobia to the rider's list of deficiencies.

On the train to London, he looked at Arthur's card. It said "Arthur J. Thomas - Man of Leisure".

The next day, Baxter was sitting in a much more comfortable mode of transport. The Roller had the numberplate DRAW 8. Baxter sat next to Arthur enjoying a Montecristo cigar and talking racing.

"You'll like Finnie" said Arthur. "He used to be a head lad at Lambourn but he's bought his own place at Epsom -

this is his first season training."

"Does he know what he's doing?" enquired Baxter bluntly.

"I hope so" smiled Arthur. "He's a betting man himself and if he doesn't get winners quickly he won't last long. Besides he's keen and it's worth giving him a chance."

They pulled into a paved yard of a dozen boxes where two lads were mucking out. The door of a small office opened and a freckle-faced man with light wavy hair wearing a quilted jacket and jodhpurs came out to greet them. He had bright green eyes and that drawn look around the mouth and nose, which is common to sons of Erin.

"A real good race she ran yesterday, Mr Thomas" he smiled " and she's come out of it well. But come now and see for yourself."

They followed Finnie to a box from which he led out the filly.

"Then you still think we can go for a touch at Folkestone on Friday?" said Arthur.

"Oh, I'm sure you can, sir. As you know we've been covering her up in her three races so far and she's well in at Folkestone. She's a bit better than selling class and there's nothing in the race. In fact, it's so poor I don't think we'll have any trouble buying her in if you want to. I'd like to keep her though" said the trainer.

"Of course, if she wins buy her in" nodded Arthur.

Finnie grinned "Oh she'll win alright - I'm sure of that much."

"That sounds very confident" remarked Baxter, already visualising the slaughter of several bookies.

"If the going is good and Jackpot doesn't win then I'll

forget all about it and join the priesthood" smiled Finnie.

Back in the car, Arthur looked across at Baxter.

"What d'you think of him?"

"I like him" said Baxter. "I'll like him a lot more if Jackpot wins on Friday."

When Baxter arrived at Folkestone, he was exceedingly overdrawn on his bank account. However, as he would have told the bank manager there was no point in smashing into the bookies with the monetary equivalent of a pea-shooter. He had also recommended maximum stakes on his tipping line service adding that Jackpot was doing press-ups after training just for fun.

It was a fine day, the going was good and the only disappointment was that the selling handicap over a mile had cut up to only six runners.

In the bar, he found Arthur looking thoughtful while Finnie chattered away in his happy style.

"Everything okay?" asked Baxter.

"T'is grand" said Finnie " and as near a certainty as I've ever had. Now what'll you be having?"

Baxter drank the whiskey, then quickly had another. A feeling of optimism enveloped him. Arthur had already had his bet on off-course because it wasn't a strong market and most bookmakers took a jaundiced view of sellers.

They stayed in the bar for the first race and then Finnie left to get the horse saddled up. Arthur pulled out his wallet.

"Put a £100 on in the ring for me" he told Baxter. "It 'll help towards buying her back in."

With his own pockets extensively upholstered for a bout of bookie-bashing, Baxter considered Arthur as under-investing

"Finnie thinks she's a really good thing."

"I know but he's a born optimist. Nice man but a bit too laid back for me" said Arthur. "Still, I've got to listen to him - that's what he's paid for."

It wasn't easy to get a lot of money on in the ring but eventually Baxter had spread it around and averaged 5-2 about Jackpot. Baxter was pleased because if the trainer was right 2's on would have been overpriced.

With six runners the draw wasn't going to matter. The field swung round right-handed on the far side with the six runners closely bunched. As they came into the straight Jackpot cruised up to join the leader with another horse making headway on the outside. These three began to draw clear and a furlong out they were all in a line. With half a furlong to go, the bats were out in earnest and still nothing to separate them. The crowd roared, Baxter's knuckles gripped white as he pressed the bins even tighter. Coming up to the line, the horses were locked together - it was going to be on the nod.

"Photo finish" came the announcement.

Baxter's legs had the supporting capability of plasticine as he made an unsteady passage to the winner's enclosure. On the way he met a grim-looking Arthur.

"What d'you reckon?" said Baxter weakly.

"It's tight - like my chest" grimaced Arthur.

Baxter agreed. He was feeling distinctly unwell himself.

In the enclosure, Finnie was putting a rug over the horse and smiling from ear to ear.

"You must have enjoyed that" he called to them.

Baxter and Arthur nodded limply. There was a crackle on the speaker as the result was announced. Jackpot was third, beaten a short head and a head.

They looked at Finnie. He was smiling that eternal smile.

"Reckon the trainers of the other two had been covering 'em up as well. Good race though, wasn't it?" he said.

TOO MUCH OF A GOOD THING

The light was fading fast as the horses entered the final furlong at Newmarket. One horse was clear and the loud cheers from the bookmakers said it all. A good result for them and being the last race of the day it meant heavy hods to haul.

Baxter tore up his ticket, threw it up in the air and, allowing it to cascade over him, looked like a bridegroom at a shotgun wedding. He glanced at the race card as the winner was announced. Baxter hadn't even considered it, the form was worthless and the horse had won at 14-1. Ashton had worked the oracle with another one, thought Baxter, referring to a trainer, who in his first season had already landed several touches. It seemed that today had been no exception for amongst the general glee in the ring two bookmakers were wailing. It was such a pleasurable sound to Baxter that despite a financially disastrous afternoon he managed a smile.

What had happened was that two of that greedy fraternity had been rash enough to mark up 25's about Ashton's horse and connections had stepped in and given them a spanking. Another bookmaker, who had escaped the mauling and was dismantling his joint, looked across.

"Serves you right, you don't take chances with Ashton - he knows the time of day."

This reprimand only increased their wailing so that a big

guy collecting his proceeds made an appeal.

"Would you mind not making the notes wet" he said.

Baxter had seen the man with Ashton at previous meetings. He was like a minder with an appearance that argued he could have stood in for King Kong without requiring make-up. He was still having money pushed into his spade-like hands when Baxter headed for the exit.

Just past the grandstand, an unmistakable dumpy figure was hanging around waiting to tap someone. Baxter usually tried to avoid Clipper, especially when he had money. This time it wasn't necessary.

"My old friend, Baxter."

An arm fastened around his shoulder with excessive warmth.

"Don't even bother to ask" said Baxter. "I never backed a winner."

"Only £20 - please!" urged Clipper. "I'll pay you back."

Clipper always added this but it was as likely as a queue at the National Death Centre. Alarmingly, it seemed to Baxter, was the fact that Clipper himself was the trainer of a small yard but was always without money and an unabashed scrounger.

"I came here today only thinking I knew things and I've done my money" explained Baxter. "But you should know things - what's wrong with you?"

"There's many a twixt" said Clipper. "Two good things I was given today, one needs another furlong and the other needs shooting. I think the bookies are paying the owner to keep running it."

"You should ask Ashton, he seems to have landed some nice bets today."

"Has he now?" said Clipper. "Well that doesn't surprise me. He's no fool that one" he called, as Baxter walked off.

Ashton was clearly earning himself a reputation as a shrewd operator and Baxter had an envious respect for trainers who landed gambles. He'd have loved to be in on them but as he seldom was, he made quite a study of anticipating their minds and forecasting their intrigue. As a tipster, Baxter relied heavily on the form-book, on his informants at various stables and on long-standing experience. Unfortunately, this tended to bias in certain racing matters.

One of these was a stout resistance to entrusting his cash to horses ridden by apprentice jockeys. However, this prejudice was now having to be rapidly re-appraised due to the riding of a young lad named Tommy Box who's riding had impressed him several times and always at great cost to Baxter's emaciated wallet. The lad had ridden the first winner at Newmarket that day and Baxter reckoned it wouldn't be long before his claim was reduced to 3lb.and that seeing him booked to ride in a handicap for an outside stable was a tip in itself.

It was early November and Baxter was sitting in his office. The letter from his bank manager was less than cordial and left Baxter convinced that he was not an esteemed customer. As he reflected on the unsuccessful flat season that was drawing to a close, the spectre of having to get a proper job loomed before him and made him feel feverish. He pulled a bottle from a drawer, poured himself a glass of Macallan, gulped it down and took a deep breath - he had to pull himself together.

He turned down a bar of the electric fire and, opening

up his Racing Post, immersed himself gently into the hope and opportunity of its pages. Baxter turned to the ante-post prices for the November Handicap, the last big race of the flat season. Finding the winner could be his salvation and with the Newmarket meeting still fresh in his mind he was getting a strong fancy for a horse of Ashton's named Whackit.

For the last week or more, the horse had been consistently nibbled at ante-post and was now 16-1. What bothered Baxter was that Whackit was set to carry 8 stone and that the stable's regular jockey named Bremner was supposed to ride. However, Baxter knew that unless Bremner followed a no-food diet, rode naked and bareback, no way could he make the weight. So if he didn't want to catch cold and look ridiculous, 6lb overweight was unavoidable and that simply didn't make sense to Baxter.

On Friday, he was still mulling over the discrepancy when he boarded the train at Kings Cross for Doncaster. He settled himself and looked at the runners and riders for the next day. Whackit was now down to 12-1 in some lists because the going was soft which it liked. What surprised him though was that Tommy Box, the apprentice 'find' of the season, hadn't any booked rides.

By Peterborough, the complexity of winner-finding began to tire Baxter and he slipped into his favourite reverie. Everything he backed won, bookmakers kept sending him fat cheques, he became a racehorse owner and landed such prodigious coups that bookies cowered at the sound of his name.

He was about to win the Derby when the train stopped at Grantham. As he opened his eyes a small boy was putting a holdall into the luggage rack. When he turned and sat down Baxter blinked.

"Tommy Box the jockey, isn't it?" said Baxter.

"That's me." The boy smiled cheerfully. "Racing man are you?"

"Sort of" admitted Baxter "I'm going to Doncaster for the meeting tomorrow."

"Me too" said Tommy.

"But you've not got any rides, I've looked in the paper."

"They don't know everything" said the youngster cryptically.

Baxter waited but Tommy obviously wasn't saying anymore because he pulled a comic from his pocket and began to read. Something was up though, decided Baxter - and it was probably something worth knowing. He invited the boy to the buffet bar. Tommy's young eyes brightened.

"Good idea, I'm starving."

Half an hour later, Baxter was wondering whether the lad was a medical freak for he appeared to have an enormous stomach for such a tiny frame. While Baxter struggled through a hamburger the texture of packing material, Tommy had locusted his way through a prawn cocktail, fillet steak with chips, Black Forest gateaux and cheese and biscuits.

By now, Baxter had made a substantial investment in the young jockey without return, the lad having been too busy eating to talk.

"I suppose you can't have a drink" said Baxter dismally. "I mean alcohol - you're too young."

"No problem" smiled Tommy. "What you do is, you order a vodka and a glass of lemonade. The barman thinks the lemonade's for me but I drink the vodka and you have the lemonade - simple isn't it?"

By the time they got to Retford, Tommy had downed his third vodka and Baxter was thoroughly sick of lemonade. The boy was peering through heavy-lidded eyes when he suddenly blurted out.

"I'm going to win the November Handicap tomorrow." He paused. "Cos I'm riding Whackit for Mr Ashton."

"Whackit!" echoed Baxter. "But Bremner's supposed to ride."

"Ah, but he's not going to" Tommy wagged a finger at Baxter and then re-directed it to his empty glass.

The bar steward dispensed another vodka and asked about a lemonade for the boy. Baxter ignored him with a belligerent look and returned to Tommy.

"Now what's Ashton up to?" he asked.

By the time Baxter supported a legless Tommy off the train at Doncaster he was privy to a very cunning piece of stroke-pulling by Ashton. What was going to happen was that Bremner would telephone the racecourse in the morning to say he was ill and couldn't ride Whackit in the big race. Ashton would then encounter Tommy Box, who just happened to be there with his equipment, and offer him the ride. So from carrying overweight - allowing for the lad's claim - Whackit would now carry less. Baxter bundled Tommy into a cab and dropped him off at the Regent Hotel where Ashton had booked the lad in to ensure his arrival.

At the St. Leger Hotel, early sun streamed through the windows of the dining hall. It was a good breakfast and Baxter observed that the sun though pleasant, didn't have enough warmth to dry out the ground. It would still be

"Baxter supported a legless Tommy off the train"

Whackit's ideal surface. He was feeling excited and optimistic about what he'd discovered on the train when suddenly he remembered the lad's condition.

The receptionist at the Regent told Baxter that Tommy had already booked out. Whether he was all right she couldn't say on account of him being sandwiched between two men who had carried him out by his armpits. Baxter put the phone down - it sounded like Ashton and King Kong.

There was a good crowd at the course and Baxter had already spotted a number of regulars including Clipper. He was so busy looking for the apprentice jockey that he walked into a brick wall - at least, that's what it felt like. In fact, it was the back of a huge man in a dark overcoat who hadn't even felt the collision. Baxter was trying to re-orientate himself when he recognised the gorilla's voice.

"We've only just got here. The little perisher was on the binge last night - stuffing himself silly and drinking vodka. We took him to the sauna and got two pounds off him. I'd like to know how he got in that state."

Baxter gulped and slunk away. From a safe distance, he looked back and saw the two men joined by Ashton and a frail-looking Tommy. It seemed the plan was still on so Baxter took some 12-1 about Whackit in the early betting. After the first race came the official announcement that T.Box, claiming 3lb, would ride Whackit. Immediately, Whackit was cut to 10's. Baxter stepped in with his maximum and it was soon clear that Ashton and his connections weren't being left behind. Bookies impersonating window cleaners kept re-chalking Whackit's price. There was a buzz in the ring - it was an ambush. The price was going down like a 1929 Wall Street share and King Kong and his companion were wading into bookies with bundles of notes.

The runners had gone down to the post and Whackit's price of 4-1 reflected a massive gamble. There was a genuine confidence about Baxter because apart from having got value, he felt certain that Whackit was the horse to be on. He would have been supremely confident if he had not seen Tommy on the way down. The boy looked pale and half-asleep on a horse that was clearly trained to the minute. Baxter just hoped it was a 'steering job' that the gamble indicated.

Two furlongs out it looked like it was. Whackit had quickened into a four-length lead with Tommy not having moved. At the furlong marker he still had the lead but now there was a danger as the top weight Clumsy Ghost took up the pursuit. With half a furlong to go the lead was down to 2 lengths. Baxter roared at Tommy, so did a thousand others. The boy sensed the danger and started to ride. Whackit responded but Clumsy Ghost was still closing.

Tommy gave Whackit a couple of slaps but the horse had no more to give as Clumsy Ghost moved alongside. Baxter felt himself sliding down the razor blade of life for he could see Tommy had no strength to lift the horse forward that bit extra. It was a photo but those near the line knew Clumsy Ghost had it by a neck.

Baxter was stunned and his mouth dry from shouting. He repaired to the bar and sat disconsolately looking like an underwriter at the Great Fire. Tommy had left his strength in the sauna and Baxter was responsible for him having to go there. It was some time before his mood improved to resignation. He drained his glass and got up.

Outside he spotted Clipper coming towards him and was about to move away when two great fists gripped the lapels of his coat and hoisted him up. He was looking very closely into eyes that resembled the windows of a pill-box.

"Are you the one who fed Tommy up and got him drunk on that train last night?" asked King Kong.

"I think you've got the wrong man" whimpered Baxter, who from his elevated view could see Ashton and Tommy close by.

"Well?" said Ashton flatly.

"It looks like him" maintained Tommy.

The big fellow's grip tightened and seeing Baxter was otherwise engaged, Clipper was about to walk by.

"Clipper!" Baxter managed to call out. The rotund figure stopped. "These men are mistaking me for someone else."

"This is Baxter" declared Clipper. "I can vouch for him."

This seemed to improve Baxter's situation and he was lowered to terra firma.

"Would you explain to them that I was with you all yesterday evening" said Baxter hoping that his desperate effort of eye-rolling was not going unnoticed by Clipper.

"That's right, you were. We played cards and you owed me twenty quid. Have you got it by the way?"

Baxter took a note from his wallet and passed it over. King Kong smoothed back Baxter's lapels, mumbled an apology and walked off.

"Worth twenty pounds to bail you out of trouble wasn't it, Baxter?" smiled Clipper.

"It was" said Baxter wiping the anxiety from his brow "I suddenly feel a lot better"

"Maybe your luck is changing" observed Clipper.

"Oh, it certainly is. Seeing the size of those fists in close-up, I reckon you could have asked for fifty pounds!" said Baxter.

ON THE HOOF

Baxter was eating a cheese sandwich, the contents of which belonged in a mousetrap. How could anyone sell such rubbish, he asked himself? However, clients of his SureFire Tipping Service were asking themselves exactly the same question and in terms of nourishment would definitely have preferred the cheese sandwich. Baxter dumped the offending item in the waste bin and opened a packet of rich tea fingers – at least, they were consistent in their goodness. Ah yes, consistency, that wonderful attribute – if only horses had it, he would be laughing. But as he kept hearing, horses weren't machines. Neither were they biscuits, thought Baxter as he bit appreciatively at the confection before applying himself to the torture of studying a new day's racing.

As he run his eyes over the form, he was of the opinion – and not for the first time - that it was very easy to fancy some of Jebb's runners. They often seemed to run with promise, giving the impression that with a drop of a couple of pounds in the handicap, they would win. However, the handicapper rarely did this and seemed to think they didn't require any more help from him. He was clearly right about this for Jebb would invariably lift one or two decent handicaps with horses who had failed to win off the same mark in lesser races. In the process, he would hand out the sort of beating to bookmakers that normally carried a police charge of GBH. Baxter himself was permanently engaged in donnybrooks with this enemy and although he had his moments he himself was normally the victim. Generally, it was a good clip round the ear but there were occasions when he had been carried away unconscious.

In consequence, it was no surprise that Baxter was a serious admirer of Jebb's ability to overcome the bookies and it was at Epsom that he got a revealing insight of the trainer's methods. One of his runners had finished close up in a 5-furlong sprint and having eased the horse to a trot, the jockey turned the horse back towards the unsaddling enclosure. As it passed close to where Baxter was standing, he saw a glint from a hoof skip into the air and fall to the turf. Both horse and jockey seemed unaware and Baxter moved under the rail to investigate. What had come off appeared to be a racing plate but when he picked it up, it felt odd. Baxter was no horseman but he did know that horses trained in heavy working shoes and usually ran their races in aluminium racing plates. What Baxter was holding was a working shoe with the fullered side coated with aluminium paint. Baxter put the shoe in his pocket and felt rather pleased with himself – he thought he might be onto something.

Although the basic qualification for all horseracing trainers was a degree in deviousness and subterfuge, the clue the shoe had given him enabled Baxter to understand some part of this craft. Perhaps, just for a change, he could put two and two together and not make three. He had long been aware that occasionally trainers ran some of their horses in working shoes and there was nothing in Jockey Club rules that didn't allow this. Indeed, they could if they

"Baxter picked up what appeared to be a racing plate"

wished, run their horses completely unshod. It had long been standard procedure with Baxter, to check in the paddock that any horse he was going to back was wearing racing plates. This wasn't very difficult because working shoes were a steely blue colour whereas the racing plates were a shiny aluminium and you could recognise this as the horses paraded in the paddock. The inference Baxter made of any horse wearing working shoes was that it wasn't 'off' and could probably do a lot better. The difference in running a particular horse in them as opposed to the aluminium plates was conjecture but Baxter's extravagant guess was that that any horse reverting to plates would suddenly feel like Pegasus.

It seemed therefore that Jebb was running many of his horses in working shoes but with the appearance of being racing plates. Then, when the horse was primed and the gamble hatched, on went the proper racing plates and the horse would find the improvement required to win. The importance of the shoe was that it wasn't enough to simply follow every gamble on Jebb's horses. Bookmakers were not averse to using Jebb's reputation as a gambling stable to clip in the price of his runners, spread the word and suck in the mugs, engendering a self-fuelling gamble that had nothing at all to do with the stable and invariably ended in failure. Baxter had discovered this to his cost.

Back in his office, he had hung the Epsom memento on the nail that had previously supported a frame of Mill Reef.

Mrs Wilbow noticed it immediately. This itself was remarkable as the sheer ugliness and shambolic appearance of the office meant that most people shut their eyes with the pain.

"Oh, you've got a horseshoe" she said.

"A lucky horseshoe, Mrs Wilbow" said Baxter more precisely "and don't I need it! I 'm hoping it's going to make quite a difference."

"It might but I doubt it" said the landlady with all the joylessness of a reverse face-lift.

Baxter was dismayed that his landlady, who believed she could talk to plants, was apparently unable to accept the tradition of a lucky horseshoe. She shuffled off, holding her feather duster and offering an occasional flick to any surface that offended her. Baxter returned to scouring the paper and reasoned that all he had to do, was to go to the meeting where Jebb had a runner and identify whether it was wearing a working shoe painted to look like a racing plate in which case he would ignore it, or whether it was wearing a real racing plate in which case he'd have a good crack. The snag was that it was virtually impossible to tell a painted shoe from the real thing once it was on the horse.

It was a bit of a *slep* from London to Redcar but Baxter's quest for winners had the keenness of a bloodhound. Jebb had a runner there that had a chance in what was a wide-open race. The animal didn't seem fancied in the betting and finished about mid-division without ever showing. Baxter fell in with the man leading the horse back to the stables.

"Jebb's travelling head lad, are you?" asked Baxter.

"That's right" smiled the man. "Groom and driver, I do the lot."

"Painting those working shoes is quite a good trick, I reckon" continued Baxter.

The man replied with an even wider smile.

"Guvnor thinks so, but I'm surprised you can tell."

"I can't unless you always leave paint on your hands" said Baxter.

The man glanced down at his hand, still grinning.

"We're a small stable – we've got to do something to get our head in front."

Baxter liked the man's friendly open manner and what he said was true –operating in the red-light district of racing wasn't easy.

"Look, what I need to know is when your horses are wearing proper racing plates. Can you do that? I'll pay you the odds to twenty quid."

"That's fine by me. My name's Martin."

Baxter introduced himself and it was all settled very quickly. Martin would signify that the horse was fitted with proper racing plates by putting his thumb in his mouth during the parade. He was also told that Jebb was invariably in attendance himself when a horse was 'off' and he wasn't at Redcar today, which was why Martin was able to talk to him freely and not be intimidated by the trainer who had a very suspicious nature.

"It still don't mean they're gonna win though" ended Martin These words were going to haunt Baxter in the coming weeks.

The first occasion to put the scheme to the test came at Catterick. There was a meeting at Epsom on the same day and being much nearer and with a far better card, Baxter was slightly disgruntled at having to go to the Yorkshire track especially when he remembered how far the course was from the railway station. However, he consoled himself with the prospect of upholstering his wallet.

He was also encouraged when he spotted the trainer there. Jebb was a slight man with a face that, had it been considerably lower, could have won first prize in an ugly knee contest. Baxter had already wandered down to the ring to see the price of the stable's runner and 12's was freely available. He didn't really fancy Hay Meadow on form but this was irrelevant as his personal judgement had hardly bought him much prosperity.

Back in the paddock, he watched as Martin appeared to suck his thumb a couple of times and always when he was out of sight of the trainer's watchful eye. Baxter went back to the ring and found the 12's only available in one place and took it. After that 10's and 8's were quickly rubbed off and it seemed Jebb's runner was certainly being sniffed at.

The scent was right, Hay Meadow run an absolute blinder and after being badly hampered in the final furlong, it was touched off close home. Baxter knew he'd been unlucky but at least he knew the scheme would work – it was just a matter of time.

Unfortunately, a similar thing had happened at Epsom when the horse he'd put on his tipping line was also beaten in a photo, so it was understandable if the following morning he looked askance at the horseshoe hanging by it's solitary nail. His landlady didn't help by asking about it.

"Not very lucky so far, Mrs Wilbow" admitted Baxter.

"Not surprised" she said flatly.

Baxter had decided to ignore the remark when his phone rang. It was a new contact in Malton to whom Baxter was giving a trial and who so far had advised five consecutive losers that had all run appallingly. By now, the information he imparted held little interest to Baxter, who was of the opinion that the man could write a book on what he *didn't* know.

Having discouraged the unwitting Prophet of Doom from any further contact, he studied the future entries. Jebb had two more runners the following week - both at Warwick - and to Baxter's frustration neither was primed to win. On both occasions Jebb had been absent and similarly, no indication from Martin. Apart from finding the trips to the northern and midland courses tiring, Baxter's travel expenses were becoming a concern and when Ascot's July meeting arrived and Jebb had one entered up, it was a pleasant surprise

As expected, it was a difficult handicap but Baxter felt quietly confident when Martin's thumb went up to his mouth. His feet almost skipped as he dodged through the crowd and into the ring. The horse named Dads Barmy was 10's and Baxter was easily accommodated. A few moments later it was generally 8's and in a strong market was sent off favourite.

It turned out to be a cracking race with Dad's Barmy and another horse seemingly locked together in the last few yards. It was going to be on the nod and Baxter was hopping around like a wasp had flown up one trouser leg and down the other. A photo was called – Baxter waited. Then the result came. There were cheers and there were groans and the loudest groan came from Baxter. Dads Barmy had been beaten a sneeze and again he knew he'd been unlucky.

Baxter's SureFire Tipping Service was also suffering from seconditis and things got even worse when yet another tilt at the ring went astray at Beverley when one of Jebb's runners was given a lamentable ride by a jockey who, Baxter reckoned, could find traffic problems in the Gobi Desert. However, he wasn't totally discouraged because Jebb's horses were actually running well but he began to feel he was battling against the Fates and his resources were getting low.

Baxter was very quiet the next day but he was not without hope as he entered his office. It was the fourth day of Glorious Goodwood – his favourite meeting – and he refused to be depressed despite having done no more than hold his own so far. He'd stopped at the bank on the way in and had removed the last cartridges from his ammunition account. He was studying the William Hill Handicap for which Hay Meadow was a runner and Baxter really fancied it. The horse had run really well at Catterick and, although this was a big step up in class, was a winner without a penalty in Baxter's mind. He decided to go out on a limb. He wasn't going to wait for Martin's signal in the parade ring because Baxter reckoned that if Jebb had done as much money as he had on the stable's recent runners then he badly needed to land a touch here. Baxter put up Hay Meadow on his tipping line and decided on a quick malt before departing for Goodwood. He was just retrieving the bottle from his desk drawer when the pinafored figure of Mrs Wilbow appeared besides him and announced "I'd like my rent, Mr Baxter."

Baxter tried to look appealing to Mrs Wilbow – an impossible achievement acknowledged by both parties.

"Mrs Wilbow, as soon as my luck changes, you will get it."

"It's not likely to change while that's up there like that"

she nodded towards the horseshoe.

"No, no" said Baxter "that's got nothing to do with it. You see, I've been really unlucky lately. In fact, I've been so near to being very lucky that I've been really unlucky."

His landlady shook her head with the sympathy people attach to the feeble of mind. There was no point in explaining to her, short head defeats, baulked in running or any other racing misfortune.

"But it *will* change, Mrs Wilbow, I know it will."

"If it don't, I'll have to do something about it" she replied.

His landlady rarely made such threatening remarks but Baxter wasn't listening. He poured his malt and rang up his only credit account that hadn't reached its limit - after taking Hay Meadows price to £50, it had. He gulped his drink, grabbed his bins and the Racing Post and was on his way.

There had been an ante-post market for the race but Hay Meadow hadn't attracted much support and had remained around 25's and it was still this price on the course. Baxter went down to the parade ring and Hay Meadow looked a picture. Martin signalled that the horse was wearing racing plates but Baxter had already assumed this and the way Hay Meadow was bucking and kicking and full of himself, it wanted to show them to everybody. Jebb was there and his screwed-up face looked nervous for it wasn't often that small trainer as himself had a horse good enough to run at the prestige meetings. He was also the owner of Hay Meadow so that when it was turned in to be mounted, there was just himself and the jockey waiting in the centre of the parade ring. There were, however, plenty of his connections in the betting ring because when Baxter looked on the boards the 25's had all gone. He got all his bet on at 20's and within a minute that had gone too. There was clearly an avalanche of money for Gay Meadow because it took a massive gamble to take it from 25's down to 8's at Glorious Goodwood. Just occasionally, bookmakers take an absolute pasting like naughty schoolboys lined up before a vicious headmaster - this was one of those wonderful occasions.

Receiving a wedge of money from the hod gave Baxter an enormous buzz. Everything was good, life was worth living – this was the effect winning big had on Baxter. His luck had finally changed.

Baxter almost danced up the steps to his office that evening. It was still light and pleasantly warm. He'd had a great day and lots of red pictures of the Queen in his wallet. He sat down, poured himself a large Macallan and lit a cigarette. As the blue haze drifted across his smiling face he re-lived the race again. Hay Meadow had come through the field like an arrowhead in the final furlong and the official winning distance of five lengths had been extended to eight in the re-thinking. Any further recalls and Baxter would have had the jockey sitting with his arms folded across his chest, grinning at his rivals as he strolled to the front. This indulgence was interrupted when Mrs Wilbow appeared at his office door.

"Come in, Mrs Wilbow" called Baxter brightly.

As she entered, he pointed to a wallet that seemed on the point of exploding. "Take what you need and a little bit more for interest" he invited her.

"I knew your luck would change" she said. She took the money and slipped it into her pocket. "Notice anything different in here?" she challenged him.

Baxter gazed around his chaotic surroundings that even a wrecking ball would have found hard to disfigure.

"No, can't say I do" he smiled.

"Well, after you left this morning I put that horseshoe the right way up. You've had it hanging down on one nail so I put another one in so that it was hanging up like a cup to keep your good luck in. When it's down like you had it, it lets all your luck run out - I thought you'd have known that."

"No, I didn't, Mrs Wilbow" said Baxter with admiration "but I'm very glad you did."

HAVING A BAD TIME

It was that most dreaded of all weekdays - a Monday - that found Baxter in a mood as black as the clouds which moved grimly past the window of The SureFire Tipping Service. The memories of a disastrous Saturday's racing remained fresh like the pain of unhealed wounds despite the intervening Sunday when his hapless spirit seemed summoned by the ringing of the bell of the local church. However, Baxter decided that he was probably beyond redemption, blocked out the noise by closing the double-glazing and went back to bed.

Apart from habit, he wasn't quite sure why he was bothering to go to his office at all. For the first time that season, he declined to pick up his racing paper from the hallway. It would only contain the obituaries of his lost bets and the thought of a new day's racing programme with which to torture his brain was rather like a shell-shocked soldier wandering back to the front line.

Like innumerable punters before him, Baxter was, in fact, waving the white flag of surrender to the lot of them: to the unpredictable horses, to the scheming trainers, to the artful jockeys, to the villainous bookies. Besides, it was such an unequal battle - a peashooter against heavy cannon, bemoaned Baxter. The reason for his normal optimism being so utterly overwhelmed was that he was truly skint or, in his own words, potless.

If only he had been born in some distant paradise where horseracing was unknown and bookmakers were merely mythical bogeymen with which to keep naughty children under restraint. Perhaps if his first-ever bet of sixpence on a 20-1 winner had never come up, his interest would have been stunted and the word 'turf' would have had no more meaning than a piece of earth with grass roots.

These regrets, however, only served to deepen his depression and he decided a walk in some fresh air might restore him somewhere near to a state of humanity. He put on his coat and went out, his head low and dejected and his eyes fixed morosely to the grey pavement.

There were many bitter memories of that black Saturday to be forgotten but the worst by far was that of his 'good thing' getting beat in a photo finish. Unfortunately, it was this very image which kept tormenting him and which again raised its ugly short head when he came across the tin can lying on the pavement before him.

Baxter couldn't help himself. He gave it a mighty kick and followed its upward trajectory until it was stopped in its path by the chest of a man about two sizes bigger than a rhinoceros. It seemed, also, that the tin had not been quite empty for a small quantity of baked beans was now dripping down from the man's shirt. Recognising the look of someone dangerously close to exploding, Baxter gulped, turned around and legged it.

The clap of heavy hob-nailed boots behind him, encouraged Baxter to achieve a below average time for two furlongs before he collapsed exhausted behind a row of dustbins. When he finally poked his head between a pile of newspapers and some plastic bottles, he was considerably

"He gave it a mighty kick"

relieved to find that his pursuer had failed to stay and was presumably tailed-off.

Baxter gripped the edge of a dustbin with both hands and, in levering himself up, discovered a surprisingly good edition of that day's Racing Post lying on top. He hesitated momentarily but the instinct was too strong and he grasped the paper like a welcome friend. Still unnerved, he felt he needed a good stiff drink but his impecunious state led him not to the Drover's Arms but instead to Toni's cafe where he sat down with a strong cup of tea.

He gazed at the paper benignly, ignored the tragic details of Saturday and reviewed the runners for today's races. It was when he turned to the card at Ayr that he let out a cry like a hare caught in a gin-trap. The name Ritz Gruel leapt out from the page for this was a horse which Baxter had been following at great cost all season and whose form figures read like a necklace of bagels.

Ritz Gruel was owned and trained by a Machiavellian character named Stobbs, who Baxter reckoned had pulled more strokes than Oxford and Cambridge put together. Baxter could see the eventual result in his mind now. Ritz Gruel would have romped in at a nice price and the trainer had been invited by the stewards to explain his improved form.

"Well it does seem the Scottish air brings out the best in my horse" Stobbs would have said "and we also tried a bit of haggis in with his corn this morning and that must have helped."

Of course, what he should roughly have said was "I have been fiddling the hindquarters off my horse all season and the reason he won today was because the money was down and he was trying."

Baxter stopped his fantasising and looked sharply up at the clock on the wall. It was ten minutes to one and Ritz Gruel was in the one o'clock at Ayr. He gulped the remains of his tea and was about to dash to the betting shop. Instead, he let out another anguished cry - no money, he remembered!

Toni, the cafe owner, was leaning on the counter being pleasantly amused by Baxter's antics.

Baxter approached with a face of desperate earnestness.

"Toni, how would you like to lend me a fiver?"

"The same as I would like to jump offa de cliff top" was the reply.

"But I only want to borrow it for fifteen minutes, then you will have it back" said Baxter.

"Now you wanna de fiver and in fifteen minutes time you no wanna de fiver. I donna understand."

Baxter cast another anxious glance at the clock before explaining.

"Look, I have this horse which I just know is going to win. The trouble is I have no money to bet with."

"Ah, so you wanna put my fiva pounds on a horse. No thanka you very much." Toni had switched his attention to some tea pools on the counter and proceeded to mop them up.

The Latin's refusal didn't surprise Baxter. English trainers were constantly popping over to Rome for a day out, plundering the big races with glorified handicappers and getting a suntan into the bargain.

"Listen" pleaded Baxter "if you lend me five pounds now, I will give you back six."

Two dark eyes abandoned the tea pools and gleamed up at Baxter.

"Fiva pounds for six?"

"Yes, but hurry up!" urged Baxter, his voice rising to a shrill pitch.

"Okay, I taka de chance with you just this once."

The note was hardly out of the till before Baxter had snatched it up and was haring off to the bookies. Providence had revealed itself in his direst hour for he just knew that this was to be Ritz Gruel's day and even the black sky was clearing as he dashed past bewildered pedestrians.

He braked to a halt outside Armstrong's, burst in, scribbled his bet and stampeded towards the counter. The clerk looked at his slip.

"I think you've backed a winner" she said.

"I hope so" said Baxter breathlessly.

"No, you definitely have" said the woman. "Unfortunately, you have to put them on before the result comes up. I know it's more difficult but it's a company rule."

Baxter gave her a vacant stare.

"That result's been up five minutes" she added wryly and pointed to a screen which showed that Ritz Gruel had won at 9-1. Baxter spluttered incoherently and then, seeing the digital clock indicating 1.10, let out a pathetic howl.

He tossed the bet away and released an hysterical laugh of a man who has just lost his mind. He didn't care where he was going but his forlorn steps led him past Toni's cafe where the proprietor was standing in the doorway.

"I see you coma back to give me my money" smiled the Italian.

Baxter's lips seemed sealed by grief as he silently stuffed the fiver into a greasy hand. When he did find his voice it was full of acrimony.

"Why don't you get a clock which shows the right time?"

Toni broke off from his quizzical study of the note.

"Ah, the clock, yes it looza de time but who cares? Wassa de ten minutes here or there? By the way, I have only the five pounds and you havva to give me six, eh?"

Baxter's stream of invective that followed was worthy of any trooper who ever lived. It was several minutes before he exhausted his unkindest vocabulary and stormed off.

The cafe owner was still reeling under the onslaught.

"Wassa de matter with him?" he asked himself. "Jussa because my clock is a fewa minutes slow."

A RARE OLD DAY

The rain fell steadily and a grey December sky gave little likelihood of it relenting. However, there was a distinct air of optimism about Baxter as he entered his office that morning. He was normally optimistic but today especially so. There was no reason for it, the SureFire Tipping Service was doing reasonably well, a few winners interspersed with the inevitable losers- nothing to warrant full-page spreads in the racing press but, there again, nothing to justify looking out for aggrieved clients wishing to remodel his face.

Yes, he felt very good indeed. He interpreted this as either an indication that he was about to hear of a good thing from his stable contacts or that he was about to uncover a stone-bonking certainty from his study of form.

Half an hour later, he had surprisingly found such an animal in the very first race - a hurdle for 3 year olds at Ascot. He was about to check on the horse's going preference when Mrs Wilbow entered and silently placed a slice of cake on a plate besides him. Baxter looked at the confection that contained cream, nuts and several dental appointments.

"It's my birthday" she smiled.

"Really?" said Baxter " I never knew that."

"Yes, March 23rd - same every year and every year you say that. For 15 years you've been saying it."

"Have I really?" said Baxter apologetically but wanting to resume his study of form.

"I'm 56" said his landlady in a tone that required a favourable denial of the fact.

"You really don't look it" obliged Baxter thinking, in fact, that she looked decidedly older.

"I do my best" she smiled. "I'm going to treat myself to the hairdresser's later."

"Well, happy birthday, Mrs Wilbow and thank you" said Baxter anxious to curtail the pleasantries and trying to remember exactly where he had been in his quest regarding the potential 'good thing'.

"Going!" he remembered aloud.

"Alright, Mr Baxter, I can see you're busy" Mrs Wilbow was clearly hurt by the remark and had gone before Baxter could explain the misunderstanding.

"Oh dear" thought Baxter, confirming to himself that he was right to avoid marital status which undoubtedly would have been sprinkled with such occurrences.

At last, he found what he wanted. The horse came from a stock of mud-lovers whose performances indicated hippopotamus in the bloodline and whose own previous wins had all been in the soft. Why look further? was Baxter's reasoning. He'd found the nugget - that was it. He put the message on-line to his subscription and premium line clients and made his preparations for the journey to Ascot.

The free local paper was on the downstairs mat as he left. He picked it up and, together with his Racing Post, thrust it into his overcoat pocket.

From the train window, he watched approvingly as fields of cows huddled together against the weather and a steady drizzle trickled down the glass.

Baxter was almost a lone figure as he watched the

"Hippopotamus in the bloodline"

runners in the first race being led around in their waterproof sheets. To add to his discomfort, there was a biting wind at the Berkshire track and he decided that win or lose he was off after the first race. Better death by a single blade than one by several cuts seemed the right policy for the rest of the card looked agonisingly hard and had attracted some unusually large fields.

What did please him, however, was that his selection, Cosmic Monk looked well, looked alert and more importantly had feet like plates - and platter size at that.

Having lumped on at 5 to 4 and 11 to 10, Baxter considered he'd done well when evens was the general call at the off. However, after a few minutes of viewing through his binoculars, Baxter wouldn't have had it at 20's for despite being a winner of its three previous hurdle races, Cosmic Monk gave a display of jumping that suggested it was trying to rearrange the fences. After hitting the first two hurdles hard, his pilot was already trying to recall the Injured Jockey's Fund's number. It made another mistake at the third before inevitably tipping over at the next to provide a unique aerial view of the course to his unfortunate jockey.

Baxter was disappointed but not as much as he would have expected. He made his way back to the station curiously sanguine. However, he had certainly had his fill of racing for the day and on the train discarded his Racing Post in favour of the local paper. Glancing through the pages, his eyes fastened on a photo showing a Lilliputian figure holding a large lollipop several inches taller than himself. The caption read 'Charles Corrigan, the patrol officer at the new crossing'. It appeared that local residents had petitioned successfully for a crossing outside a local school and that 'Corker' Corrigan, ex-jockey and serial stroke-puller, was its custodian.

Well, well, thought Baxter smiling, to think the old rogue was living locally. 'Corker' Corrigan had been a decent jockey at one time with a unique but ugly all-action style. He was often able to cover horses up or even stop them but not always with the trainer's connivance - an oversight they didn't appreciate. He was a bit of a nightmare for stewards and trainers because his jockeyship was constant motion implying great effort but often concealing the object of getting the horse unbalanced.

On the other hand, canny trainers would use him to slip in unfancied horses using the same ungainly style. Corrigan could ride all right but he was consistently unreliable and so tricky he could walk through a thunderstorm and not get wet.. But to Baxter, 'Corker' Corrigan was a source of great fondness because he'd helped the jockey in the illegal practice of placing bets for him. Baxter felt no remorse for this, it went on all the time and if he hadn't obliged someone else would have. The great thing about Corrigan was that he rarely made mistakes with his mounts and Baxter had benefited from the information both privately and occasionally - when it needed an uplifting winner - through his tipping service.

It had gone well for a few seasons but the jockey eventually became careless, started to get a few suspensions, trainers and owners decided his association was best avoided and the rides simply dried up. 'Corker' Corrigan had drifted out of racing as imperceptibly as he had entered.

It was near school-leaving time when Baxter got off the train at his local station. By now, he'd decided he wanted to renew acquaintance with the ex-jockey and made his way towards the school. 'Corker' was there shepherding the flocks of children and their parents across the road and seemed delighted when Baxter greeted him with an arm around the shoulder.

In between the passages of ferrying, Baxter learnt 'Corker' had moved down to London because of his wife who was a 'townie'. He'd taken the job of 'lollipop man' because he liked kids and having a few quid in the bank he didn't need to work much.

They reminisced long after the last trickle of kids had left the school and Baxter had enjoyed it. He exchanged telephone numbers with 'Corker' and had made a potentially valuable contact because 'Corker's' son was now employed in a Middleham stable and was described by his father as 'chip off the old block'. For Baxter's purposes there was no higher praise.

He made his way back to the office. It was now late afternoon and the light was fading. He pulled his collar up against the wind. It was still raining and yet he still had that cheerful equanimity with which he had started the day. It was odd because normally the plunge on Cosmic Monk would have extinguished it decisively but it remained quite unmoved by the setback. Besides, renewing acquaintance with 'Corker' had been fun and days couldn't be valued simply by monetary gain or loss, Baxter convinced himself.

It was in this healthy but temporary frame of mind that saw him approach Armstrong's betting shop. Baxter had no further interest in racing for the time being and yet his legs seemed to propel him through the door and deposit him in front of the bank of TV screens in the shop. He looked at the runners for the last race at Ascot and one of the names caught his eye. Then he peered into his wallet which revealed a solitary tenner. What was the point?

Mrs Wilbow heard the abrupt knock on her door. She peered tentatively through the gap and then opened it wide.

"Oh Mr Baxter" she murmured touching her hair.

"It looks very nice."

Baxter meant it and he smiled. Suddenly he produced the flowers, which he had been holding behind his back.

"Happy Birthday, Mrs Wilbow" he said.

"Oh-h-h Mr Baxter, they're beautiful." His landlady was quite overcome. "I suppose your horse won" she said perceptively.

"Actually that horse didn't but a little while ago another one did and it was 40-1!"

"Well, thank you for the flowers" said the landlady "I've had a really lovely day."

"And so have I" replied Baxter. "I just had this comfortable feeling right from the start."

He turned away chortling to himself. "What a winner! Birthday Cake! I had to do it! But 40-1! What a winner!"

MESSAGE RECEIVED AND UNDERSTOOD

Baxter was at Chester's May meeting. He liked the city and he loved the racing at the Roodeye. However, he didn't always like the results. He removed the betting ticket from his pocket and crumpled it with the disgust an opera buff would dispense to an invitation to a karaoke night. He then tossed it into the air and kicked it into a velocity that far exceeded anything shown by the animal it represented.

"Hey Baxter, how would you like a mobile phone?"

He looked around to see Freddie Compton, a retired man, always at the races and the owner of a couple of moderate handicappers. He was showing off a slim, silver grey model.

Baxter response to modern technology was very slow and reluctant and he only indulged it when absolutely necessary, as was the case with the telephone and recording equipment required to run the SureFire Tipping Service. He now managed to operate the stuff but fiddling about with electrical and mechanical devices was not his cup of tea and he received Freddie's offer with the enthusiasm of a dog being prepared for a walk on Guy Fawkes Night.

"No thanks" replied Baxter "never really fancied one."

"Look, it's free. I'm giving it to you" urged Freddie.

"So why don't you want it?"

"It's unlucky to me" sighed Freddie. "This phone is an absolute *boch*."

Superstition played a part in the perception of many racegoers but Freddie had taken it to excess. He had once worn a pink carnation in his lapel and backed so many winners that day that he kept wearing it until the flower started to wilt. Freddie's luck had remained good and he did everything to keep the moribund flower alive even spraying it with hair lacquer to keep it together. Eventually, it disintegrated to the point where people were asking him why he was wearing a stalk pinned to his lapel. Even now, Freddie would reminisce about the pink. "What a carnation that was!" he'd recall.

"So why should I want a *boch* phone?" Baxter's response was perfectly reasonable.

"It's a *boch* to me but maybe not to you. Take it please" implored Freddie. "The first call I got on it was from my wife telling me she was leaving me after 40 years of marriage – do you believe that!"

"I'm sorry to hear that, Freddie" offered Baxter.

"Ah, that wasn't so bad" said Freddie dismissively "anyway I always wanted to tell her she was a lousy cook. No, the worst thing is that I can't back a winner since I've had it."

He thrust the phone into Baxter's hand.

"Take it! Get a charger for it and you're away"

He walked off, calling back "Be lucky!" which seemed inappropriate after giving someone a jinx phone.

After leaving the course and walking along Watergate Street to the city centre, Baxter was reflecting on a successful afternoon. He'd had a good bet on the winner of the last race and his only major disappointment was the failure of the horse he'd put up on his tipping line, which had handled the track with the same manoeuvrability as a steamroller in a chicane.

Never mind, there was another day tomorrow and it was in this optimistic frame of mind that he remembered the phone. His previous stance of complete indifference to mobile phones was now under siege from the simple fact that he now actually owned one.

He conceded to this interest and popped into a shop where a young lad sold Baxter a charger, fitted a new card and patiently showed him how to operate the thing. Despite the lad's thick Lancashire accent, he didn't find it too difficult and felt rather pleased with his new acquisition.

Baxter had planned to be at Chester for the second day but this was sabotaged shortly after his morning shower when a dull explosion occurred in the region of his boiler. Shortly after, there was a 'pop' and he realised he had no electricity. As the phone no longer worked, Baxter resorted to his mobile and arranged for a plumber and electrician to call that afternoon.

Baxter knew that his demanding subscribers would expect a tip for the feature race of the day, the Chester Cup. However, his domestic disaster meant that there just wasn't sufficient time to make a thorough study of the race and there was no encouraging information from his contacts. However, Baxter was a great believer in horses and people that were 'in form' and he knew that 'Bendex' in the Daily Express was having a blinding run. It was therefore this hack's selection that Baxter offered to his subscribers.

It was the most gratifying part of the afternoon when the horse obliged and somewhat eased the pain of the hideous bill the two tradesmen presented him with.

The shrill, unfamiliar sound in his pocket startled Baxter for a moment but he then remembered the mobile – it was his first incoming call.

"Ah, you're there then Baxter. Didn't see you at Chester today – thought you might have fallen under a bus."

"Eh?" mumbled Baxter.

"The *boch* phone. Thought you might have had a disaster." It was Freddie Compton.

"No, in fact, I gave out the winner of the big race."

"I backed it too! I should have dumped that phone weeks ago. I've told everyone I'm no longer on it so you won't get any calls for me. Anyway, I'm glad you're okay, I was feeling guilty!" He laughed and rang off.

Thursday was a hectic morning for Baxter. He'd got in early to his office to study form before leaving for Chester. Having sorted out a good thing, he then had a strong message from a Newmarket source for the same animal. His confidence fortified, he not only recorded it for his clients but made an additional trip to the bank for some readies to back it with on course.

He was just about to leave for Euston when Mrs Wilbow entered with her broom.

"You off are you? You do have a lovely time of it."

"Yes, going to Chester. You might see me on the tele" joked Baxter.

"Would you wave to me?" she said gently.

Baxter knew then that Mrs Wilbow was in one of her feeling-sorry-for-herself moods.

"I suppose, I could but how will I know when you're watching?" said Baxter somewhat alarmed at the idea.

"I could telephone you on that mobile phone you've just

got." said Mrs Wilbow. "Would you?"

Baxter had forgotten that in a bout of sub-conscious exuberance he had mentioned his new possession. Baxter scribbled down the number.

"Okay ring me if you want to." He then left before Mrs Wilbow's play-acting made him do anything else silly. Any more of it and he might have brought her rent up to date, he thought.

The further north the train went, it was clear that what had been a light morning drizzle in London was becoming steady downpour. At Chester General, brooding clouds were still chucking it down and at the course the going had been officially changed to soft.

Baxter headed straight for the bars to get a drink inside him. There was a good crowd but the festive spirit had been severely diluted by the weather. Baxter's own disposition, considerably buoyed by the belief that his good thing would win, had been breached by the sudden change in the going and finally scuppered by the announcement that the animal was to be a non-runner.

His mood wasn't improved by the appearance of Yates and a couple of his cronies in the bar. Of all the characters he knew in racing, he was the only one he disliked personally. There were plenty he didn't trust or respect. He didn't like bookies but only as a group and simply because they were the enemy. The same went for trainers because they were always plotting and, more to the point, they never told him the plot.

Yates was different because he was a naturally nasty piece of work. He was a short man in his forties with a high forehead, narrow eyes and a hooter that could have decorated a parrot. His mouth was a narrow slot bordering two rows of uneven yellowing teeth and his skin stretched across his face with a hue ranging between red and mauve. In short, it was a face that could frighten a corpse. Despite his stature, he was loud and confident which contradicted the nervous tensions in his face – the twitching of his eyebrows and lines suddenly appearing on his brow.

What interested Baxter, however, was the fact that Yates had the ear of several gambling trainers and executed commissions on their behalf. Wherever Yates was, a plot was never far away. Years before, Yates had accused Baxter of putting up a horse for which he had a stable commission and of ruining the price. Baxter just happened to have his own contact in the stable and knew nothing about Yates' instructions. Baxter wasn't bothered but the pair had never spoken to each other since.

Outside, large puddles had formed across the tarmac and when Baxter did venture out he looked around for someone who might know something. It seemed, though, that most people had decided to hole-up out of the rain and Baxter felt that his hefty wedge of cash was likely to remain intact. Besides, he didn't like betting on heavy going considering it to throw up too many surprises.

By the time of the fourth race, Baxter had had at least two whiskies more than normal and seemed to be consoling himself for the weather and for his tip being a non-runner.

He was now in the bar nearest the paddock, pushed his way to the counter and found himself in a cramped space behind Yates who, this time, hadn't noticed him. Baxter had quite forgotten about Mrs Wilbow when his mobile gave a subdued ring from inside his pocket.

"You'll have to speak up, I can't hear you very well" he

"Large puddles had formed across the tarmac"

shouted, recognising her voice.

She was asking why she hadn't seen him on the TV and why he hadn't waved. Baxter pointed out the weather conditions but she, in turn, pointed out that he'd promised.

"Okay, when they show the horses being paraded, look out for me.......yes, yes, I'll wave." It was moments like these when Baxter understood why he'd never got married.

He finished his drink, put his hand on his hat and prepared to nudge his way through the crowd. As he did so, he realised he was about to leave his mobile behind and snatched it up.

Baxter was very self-conscious about his debut on British television and tried to appear casual as he took up several positions around the paddock. However, as the rain was still bucketing down and there were only about a dozen people present, his waving to the camera clearly identified him as an attention seeker.

Deciding enough was enough, Baxter moved off to end a short and embarrassing TV career. When his mobile phone rang again he assumed it was Mrs Wilbow but not only was there no voice at the other end but the loud ringing continued. Baxter was momentarily puzzled until realising the sound was coming from another pocket. When he located it he found himself holding two identical phones. He wasn't sure what to do but answered it and just listened.

The voice on the other end was loud and gruff and had clearly been withheld from the expense of elocution lessons.

"We knew it was a two-horse race" the voice began "but from what we've heard, we're convinced Duke of Scarecrows is the one. He'll like the ground, that's certain. Get on ten big ones at any price down to four to five."

The call was ended and Baxter still hadn't said a word.

When Baxter entered the bar again a little later, the air was loud with the noise of people shouting into each other's faces. Yates was making more noise than anyone.

"I dunno what happened. I know they fancied it but they were supposed to ring. They won't be very happy but what can I do? Good price, too, ten to eleven – could 'ave 'ad evens."

Baxter had manoeuvred himself behind Yates again. He listened to a bit more of Yates' bleating before bending down and then suddenly holding up a phone. He pushed himself into the middle of Yates' group

"Anyone lost a mobile phone?" asked Baxter.

"Where d'you find that?" said Yates snatching it from Baxter's hand.

"On the floor" said Baxter, quite unperturbed as Yates' eyes narrowed in on him.

As he turned away, he heard someone say "Wasn't that the bloke in the paddock who kept waving to the camera?"

Baxter didn't stop to confirm this because he'd also heard the 'weighed in' announcement and was off to collect a lot of money from the ring. He rather hoped he might meet Freddie Compton on the way and thank him for the mobile. Yes, thank him – that really would surprise him.

TWO DAYS TO THE MOON

Baxter's current relationship with Lady Luck was at its zenith. She had fluttered her eyelids and twirled her skirt at him to such an extent that he was producing winners at random. The formbook was abandoned to gather dust and his stable information, which had become very sparse, was not missed at all. Baxter was simply relying on his fancy and the lady was flattering him with winners as big as 8's, 10's and even a 20-1. Subscribers to the SureFire Tipping Service were amazed and one person wrote in, rather indelicately, to inquire whether the business was under new management.

Baxter had, in fact, built up a considerable betting bank from the successes but knew from previous experience with the lady that her caprices were unexpected and often ruinous. The trick was to enjoy her to the full before she dumped you.

The Middle Park Stakes at Newmarket's October meeting was to be the biggest test of the Lady's affection because Baxter was going all out for the unbeaten 2-year-old colt named Catch the Pork. Baxter was there, lumping on all his betting bank and a bit more. He averaged 7-4 and saw the horse start at 11-8. The Lady, it seemed, was still sweet on him.

What happened in the race was that having cruised to the front and stolen a two-length lead, the jockey of Catch the Pork stopped riding and had been collared on the line and beaten a sneeze in a photo. Baxter wasn't surprised but disappointed that on his most important date the Lady had dumped him in favour of the bookmakers who seemed to have an irresistible charm for her favours.

It was back to the fundamentals of hours studying the formbook and badgering his contacts for information but there followed such a long losing run that his winning streak felt like it had taken place in a previous life. It was getting Baxter down so that he had become uncharacteristically moody. Having Mrs Wilbow sweep and dust the office while he pored over his formbooks didn't normally bother him but it did now. Besides, he didn't need his office cleaned, just exorcised.

Baxter glanced at his watch. There were two meetings that day – Sedgefield and Exeter – but he declined to go on account of his appalling run and a malnourished wallet. What he did was to put up a horse in the 2.30 at Exeter to his SureFire Tipping Service subscribers with rhetoric that was totally fraudulent. In desperation, he had promised to 'join up if it didn't win' and, not really fancying a military career, was a little uneasy as he rang his bookmaker for the result.

"Toxic Soup run, did it?" he emphasised.

"Yes, sir, unseated its rider at the first fence" came the reply.

"That jockey could fall out of an electric chair" responded Baxter slamming down the phone with considerable feeling.

After a momentary thought, he excused himself of the promise to his subscribers by suggesting – quite rightly - that he would not have passed the Army medical. However, he knew this wouldn't stop the anticipated multitude of letters addressed to 'Private Baxter'.

He put the formbooks away and sighed. There was no information coming in and yet someone, somewhere, must know something. Baxter had an exaggerated view that there was at least one plot going on every day at every race meeting. The frustration was that he never got to hear about them. He decided he needed a drink to lift his spirits and it then occurred to him that there was no better place for information of any sort than the pub.

He picked up his racing paper, put on his hat and gliding silently past his landlady with just a smile, he emerged onto the street. He avoided his own pub, the Drover's Arms, feeling that he needed to seek fresh fields for information and, instead, made his way to a pub with the unlikely name of Slug and Lettuce, which had recently opened further down the High Street.

On the way, it occurred to Baxter that in devoting his entire time to horseracing and the study of it, he must have missed a new traffic law, which confined cyclists to ride on pavements instead of roads. It didn't seem very sensible to him as yet another bike brushed past his legs.

Baxter entered the pub and decided that to ask for Macallan, his favourite single malt, would be a bit like asking the local fish and chip shop for kippered salmon. Instead, he ordered the only malt available. Following an arrow that pointed 'To the Beer Garden', he found himself in a car park with some hanging baskets. Distinctly unimpressed. he went back into the pub and wandered between several different groups, none of which seemed friendly or showed any interest in him. He sat down disconsolately at a table and pulled out his paper. He'd already read it pretty thoroughly and soon put it back in his pocket. He looked around the bar for some diversion and noticed another sign reading 'Lively Atmosphere' – this he mischievously interpreted as fights at the weekend.

He wished now that he'd gone to his own pub and got up to leave. As he neared the door, he noticed three men at the end of the bar, huddled together like conspirators in a medieval intrigue.

"Days to the Moon is the fastest thing on four legs" said one of them.

Baxter braked to a halt behind them.

"He won his last race half the track" said the second "and the trainer said he's an absolute cert to win next time out."

The men's voices were low and Baxter was straining to hear. He leaned back a little more and could have done with having his shoes nailed to the floor.

"When's his next race?" asked the third man.

This was it. Baxter leaned further backwards but his state of imbalance could last no longer and he crashed to the floor.

"Right, e's 'ad enuf" said the barman leaping over the counter.

"But I've only had one whisky" complained Baxter, objecting to being manhandled.

"Yer can't hold yer spirits then, can yer?" said the barman, dumping him outside.

Back in his office, Baxter was puzzled that he hadn't heard of Days to the Moon although it was possible he'd missed it or it ran on the all-weather which Baxter didn't follow seriously. It was when he looked through the list of future runners that he found it. The horse was indeed an all-weather horse and was entered up at Wolverhampton in two days time. The trainer of the animal was a man named Benson based in Epsom. This interested Baxter greatly for in regard to skulduggery and treachery Benson was an arch exponent who, when deciding on a career, had just given the verdict to horseracing over politics.

The following day, Baxter was travelling down on an early train to check out the equine flyer named Days to the Moon for with such an apparent good thing he decided to see the horse for himself. According to what he'd heard in the pub, the horse was the sort of certainty that compared with death and taxes.

He arrived at Epsom Downs station and having walked a couple of miles and reminded himself to give up smoking, he found himself at the training gallops. There were several horses in the distance and a man, leaning against the side of a Jaguar car, had his binoculars trained on them.

"Excuse me" said Baxter "but is that some of Benson's string out there?"

"It most certainly is" said the man, not removing his binoculars.

"D'you know which one is Days to the Moon?" asked Baxter eagerly.

"I'll say I do, you can't miss it. It runs like a goat – the one at the back of the string."

Baxter raised his binoculars and focused on a skinny, long-legged chestnut toiling in the rear.

"But I've got a tip for that horse" said Baxter in disgust. "I was told he's a certainty at Wolverhampton tomorrow."

"Well, someone's been pulling your leg then. That horse will never win a race –it's useless."

"Leaning against the side of a Jaguar with binoculars to his eyes"

"But I thought he won his last race half the track" argued Baxter.

"I don't know who told you that. Last time out, it was last of seven and was so late finishing his horse-box driver had to lock up behind him!"

Baxter was both confused and crestfallen and the man could see it.

"Look, if you want a winner tomorrow, back Cobbled Motorway. It's not a certainty so don't go mad but it will run a big race. Besides, I know Benson's backing it. As for Days to the Moon, all it's good for is 500 tins of dog food. And you can quote me – I'm the owner."

With that the man turned and got into his car.

The following afternoon, Baxter was celebrating breaking his long losing run. He'd been a long time in the wilderness and poured himself a 10-year-old Macallan from the bottle in his desk. Cobbled Motorway had gone in at a decent price at Kempton, his subscribers were temporarily appeased and his confidence was restored. As for Days to the Moon, he had taken a step nearer the knacker's yard and finished last again.

As he enjoyed the sweet, malty, gingery sensations that danced about on his palate, he still couldn't understand what the three men in the pub had been up to. He could only surmise that they were paid accomplices of local bookmakers whose object was to entice innocent victims like himself to back worthless tips. However, even though Baxter believed that no foul deed was beyond them, he had to concede that this was fairly unlikely.

It was a couple of days later that the mystery was solved. Baxter was browsing through his Racing Post when he came across a headline which read 'Days To The Moon Wins Like A Champion', and underneath the story began ' Backers of favourite Days to the Moon never had an uneasy moment, for leading from start to finish he scorched round the track in a new record time of 28.48 for 475m.'

It was a report of the greyhound meeting at Walthamstow the previous night.

THE FEMININE TOUCH

To the random observer, Queen Neptune was a rather attractive bay filly. The Stud Book even had her classified as a racehorse although this was a masquerade because she never raced - at least, she didn't on the track which was where she was supposed to. She might trot, canter or even get into a working canter but race she did not. The exasperating thing about her was that she had impeccable breeding and as a yearling had cost 200,000 guineas at the Newmarket Sales.

She'd been sent to the small yard of Doug Sinclair at Middleham who was so staggered at his good fortune that he bought two lottery tickets the next day. However, Lady Luck had clearly paid only a fleeting visit as not only were the numbers unsuccessful but his Range Rover got a double puncture on the way back. This took a bit of doing and the incident was portentous.

Initially, Queen Neptune was the darling of the stable and Roddy, the lad in charge of her, absolutely adored her.

"She's going to be a star, guv" he repeatedly told the trainer "it's like driving a Formula 1 car."

Although, as he only drove a beaten-up Hillman Imp it wasn't apparent how he could know this.

However, she was clearly the best of the 2-year-olds in the yard and Roddy would just toy with the others in any serious work. As the flat season opened, the trainer realised he had something special in Queen Neptune. Work watchers were beginning to notice her on the gallops and word was getting around that Queen Neptune was one to keep an eye on when she made her racecourse debut.

She was first entered for a 6-furlong race at Newbury and in her final piece of work she had raced against a 3-year-old sprint handicapper who was decidedly useful. Roddy came back smiling from ear to ear.

"I could have taken him anytime - she's brilliant."

The trainer then knew for sure that he had something to go to town with and a top jockey was engaged for her racecourse appearance.

The aftermath consisted of a lot of head-shaking and disbelief. Queen Neptune had gone off at evens, looked to be cantering all over the others but produced nothing when asked and ran in at the back of the field.

This was the start to a pattern of races involving Queen Neptune. She always started favourite simply because of everything about her. Seeing her in the paddock, you simply couldn't oppose her. Aside from her breeding, she possessed a most captivating appearance. She had a glorious head, the most wonderful walk and, like her name implied, a regal presence. It was like watching a mannequin parading with charladies.

In her races, though, she continued to run abysmally. Different jockeys were tried, different courses, soft ground, firm ground, many punters were beginning to feel she'd be best suited underground. She was getting a reputation as a morning glory and while her star began to fade fast within the stable, it was at its apogee among bookmakers.

Indeed, Queen Neptune was held in such affection by

them that several were known to keep a photo of her in their wallets alongside the wife and kids. She was an enigma to her frustrated trainer and to Roddy, who rode her in all her work and continued to believe in her.

This then was the background to the arrival in Baxter's office of an elderly, well-groomed gentleman.

"Are you the proprietor of the SureFire Tipping Service?" he asked pleasantly.

Baxter was normally wary of this question on conservation grounds but he noted the smile and relaxed. Besides this was a particular propitious time for Baxter and he had given out four winners on the bounce.

"I am indeed, sir. Have a seat." He removed some old boxes and a congealed cup of coffee to reveal a chair. He dusted the seat with his hand, looked ashamed at the blackened member and immediately went to the sink to rinse it off. "It's the cleaner's fault - she's been off sick" said Baxter.

"And clearly for some time" said the old boy looking around at the sort of disorder normally found in a junk shop.

Baxter smiled the remark away as his visitor lowered himself into the chair.

"The reason I am here is to repay you a debt of gratitude."

"Really?" said Baxter, extending his pasteurised hand. "I'm Baxter and I'm pleased to meet you."

"Well, Mr Baxter, I joined your tipping service just a week ago and I have won £40,000 thanks to you."

"That's very good" said the astonished Baxter, thinking he might have misheard the amount.

"Several were known to keep a photo of her in their wallets"

"Of course, I realise it should have been more but I only had £2000 on the first one."

"Only two thousand" repeated Baxter taking a gulp.

"Yes, faint-hearted I suppose but the second one you said was 'a nailed-on certainty' so I had five thousand on it."

Baxter regarded the man with amazement. Usually, this description resulted in the horse running as if nailed-down.

"With the third one, I think you used the phrase 'Can't get beat - fill your boots'. Such wonderful assurance. And then, of course, there was yesterday's tip 'the biggest certainty since death' you said. 'If this gets beat, I'm the Bishop of Rome'.

"And how much did you have on it?" enquired Baxter gently.

"With that sort of guarantee, I had ten thousand on it" said the old boy forcefully.

"Ten thousand! You put £10,000 on Pussyfoot!"

Baxter's mind was reeling. At least, it explained the unexpected short prices of the horses. This lunatic had been ploughing into them like they were prophecies from Moses.

"Well, how could I lose? You're a genius, Mr Baxter."

Baxter had seldom felt so good. His self-esteem was rocketing. Perhaps he was a genius, he mused. But he then recalled having trouble spelling Musselburgh earlier and modestly demoted himself to minor genius.

"How would you like to own a horse?" added the old gentleman.

"I'd love to" replied Baxter.

"That's good because I'm retiring to Florida this weekend and I'm arranging for you to assume ownership of my horse Queen Neptune. Perhaps you remember her?"

"Uhm, I do" said Baxter with the air of someone recalling breaking their leg.

"Oh, I no she was a bit of a disaster as a 2-year-old but she missed last season through injury and she's still in training. Her lad idolises her - says she's catching pigeons in her work."

Baxter assumed they must have been carrier pigeons ferrying uranium.

"Take her" the owner went on. "Even if she's no good she's still worth a few bob as a brood mare."

Baxter had always wanted to own a racehorse and as the old boy got up from his chair, he grasped his hand.

"Thank you, you're very kind" he said.

"She's still trained by Mr Sinclair at Middleham - I'll get him to ring you and get things sorted out" said the benefactor. He gave a final glance around the room as he prepared to leave. "It's curious how with all your success you don't appear more prosperous."

"Yes, well I backed Queen Neptune a few times" explained Baxter.

His visitor gave a broad smile and left. Baxter stood at the window and watched the chauffeur-driven saloon pull away. He took a deep breath and said.

"Racehorse owner, that's me!"

Baxter had registered his colours and his silks were lying on the desk. The design was a huge red phone on white and across the front was the word 'SUREFIRE' also in red. It was quite an additional expense to the £180 a week training costs so a regular stream of winners and an extremely patient Mrs Wilbow was going to be required.

Baxter travelled to Middleham, still in the first flush of

enthusiasm as an owner and clutching the parcel containing his silks. In appearance, Queen Neptune was, as always, sheer quality. He watched her on the gallops, admired her clean, easy action and felt a wave of optimism when Roddy said she'd never felt better. But the trainer had been here several times before. He suggested they put the horse in a couple of bumper races to be ridden by his 17 year-old son who would ride for nothing. Baxter had seen him ride before and reckoned he was still overpricing himself.

Queen Neptune made her first appearance in Baxter's colours at Newmarket in a race over a mile. Baxter had no thought of backing her and he was glad he hadn't. Showing little interest, she trotted along at the back of the field the whole way. The rider, though, with kicking legs and flailing arms gave all the appearance of having a fit on the unconcerned animal.

"Stupid horse and stupid colours" said his frustrated pilot in the unsaddling enclosure.

Baxter felt dismayed, particularly at the reference to his silks, which he considered rather good.

"What's the answer, Roddy?" he asked as the rug was put over her.

Roddy shook his head. "Beats me, Mr Baxter. She goes like a dream for me at home but on the course she won't go a lick. I've done loads of horses but she's the best - I thought she'd be top class."

While he kept her, Baxter knew he'd always be working class.

They tried her again three weeks later but the result was the same and the final ignominy was that the trainer's son declared he didn't want to ride her again. It seemed the best place for Queen Neptune was at stud but Baxter liked being an owner even if the animal was unworthy and expensive. It was over his second malt whiskey in the Drover's Arms that Baxter had an idea.

The beauty of it was that he could also go for a touch with Queen Neptune because such was her reputation that she was completely ignored by bookmakers who marked her up at 50's or 66's as a matter of course. A coup was not going to require much financing. This was just as well because Baxter's bank manager regarded his account in much the same way as a gastronome would regard a plate of jellied eels.

The trainer liked Baxter's idea and the planning began. Queen Neptune was entered in a 1m 6f bumper race at Newbury. On the day, there were 14 runners and, as expected, the bookies priced her at 50's initially. Baxter was patient and one or two marked up 66's. Then, at a synchronised moment, Baxter and some of the stable staff cracked into Queen Neptune. The bookies wondered what hit them and within moments she was down to 12's.

There was a hubbub about the ring. Would the layers take a beating or would the venture end up in that huge depository marked 'Failed Gambles'?

The answer was that Queen Neptune whistled in by 10 lengths and if the beating the bookies took had been to their bodies rather than their hods they'd have been rushed to intensive care.

"I'll be called in by the stewards to explain his improved form" said the delighted trainer embracing Baxter "but who cares! I'll tell them the horse would never go for anyone but Roddy so we got him an amateur's licence and put him up."

“And the beauty is that it’s the truth” smiled Baxter.

“As long as I can ride her, she’ll win more races Mr Baxter” added Roddy.

“Yes but today was the day. We knocked ‘em cold! What a touch!”

He walked off to the ring to collect.

“What a touch!” he kept repeating.

PARROT FASHION

From his office window, Baxter watched the serene figure of the vicar walking along the street. The man smiled warmly to all those he passed and bestowed especial inspiring greetings to those who were also members of his congregation. Unfortunately, this would not have included Baxter who could have done with some inspiring in his effort to compose an encouraging message to the few remaining subscribers to his SureFire Tipping Service.

Baxter envied the vicar's untroubled demeanour – a man unpolluted by the world and free from greed, selfishness and lies. Maybe he should have joined the cloth himself, he reflected, revealing the absurdity he indulged in when his luck was out. He wasn't a bad bloke, he told himself - compared to trainers, he probably came out as a holy man. Despite this exalted self-appraisal, he couldn't quite bring himself to ask for divine help in his search for a winner. Had he done so, he reckoned he was 2's on for a knock-back, although any celestial bookmaker offering such odds would surely have been trampled in the rush to get on.

Baxter went back to his desk and sat down. He gazed thoughtfully at the abundance of bills that littered his desk, many of them shrieking for attention in bold red type. It was not an unusual situation for he had simply hit a patch where he was completely out of form and his various contacts were proving as useful as a lead life-belt..

The familiar tread of the postman on the stairs brought a moment of hope and he watched the single envelope slide down from the letterbox. He picked it up and opened it. Instead of the hoped-for cheque there was a letter from an existing client that described Baxter's tipping ability in such strong, colourful language that any decent libel lawyer would have been champing on the bit. However, he had to concede there was some justification for the complaint. He walked wearily back across the office and suddenly let out a yell. After hopping precariously around the room for a moment he could see that he'd stubbed his toe on a small picture frame that was propping up an unequal leg of his desk. He grabbed the offending object and turned it over to find himself looking at an affectionate but unattractive photo of his Aunt Ethel.

He recalled how having received it as a birthday gift from his aunt several years ago and dismantling it in a vain search for any accompanying cash, he had placed it in disgust under the desk leg. However, the refreshed memory of his Aunt Ethel also reminded him that apart from not being short of a few bob, she also had an unaccountable soft spot for her nephew.

Overcoming, his natural reluctance to go visiting senile relatives, Baxter decided that a visit to his aunt could well be worthwhile. He left a 'no selection today' message for his subscribers which he had no doubt would be received with shouts of "Alleluiah!" and planned his travel arrangements to the old lady's address in Essex.

Such was his optimism when he arrived at Hornchurch station that he invested in an expensive bunch of flowers and began practising a broad, ingratiating, smile which he still hadn't quite mastered when he rang the bell of the cottage. His aunt opened the door and squinted curiously at him through her glasses.

"It's me, your nephew William" said Baxter thrusting forward the flowers.

She touched her glasses. "Of course, William, how nice to see you."

Baxter kept smiling and entered the lounge where he immediately met the gaze of a seedy discoloured parrot perched on a chromium stand.

"Hello, silly billy" cried the parrot.

"You see, he remembers you William" said Aunt Ethel fondly.

"Uhm" mumbled Baxter, trying hard to hide his dislike of the bird which was both long-standing and mutual.

His aunt excused herself while she went off to make some tea.

"I hope the purpose of your visit is not to borrow money" she called from the kitchen.

Baxter sounded like a punctured balloon.

"Eh, of course not, Aunt Ethel."

"Yes it is, yes it is" squawked the parrot.

Aunt Ethel returned with a tray of tea.

"You see, William, I thought you may have heard of my little winnings from the bookmaker."

Baxter was pleasantly surprised to hear that his aunt had some interest in racing.

"Marvellous" said Baxter "I didn't know you gambled."

"Well, it's not gambling really, not when you know the winners in advance. I almost feel as if I'm cheating." She passed Baxter a cup and a slice of cake. "Still, I haven't been

"A seedy discoloured parrot perched on a chromium stand"

greedy. I've bought some new curtains and covers and, of course, a new stand for Peregrine."

Baxter thought that such an awful name was well deserving of the bird but turned his attention back to his aunt.

"Not getting information, are you?" he joked.

"I suppose I am" said his aunt. "And so far it has never been wrong" she added smugly.

Baxter would normally have dismissed such claims of his aunt as whimsical imaginings of a decaying mind but just now he regarded anyone who could back winners as some sort of messiah.

"I suppose you don't know the winner of the 3 o'clock at Towcester today?" asked Baxter earnestly. This particular race was a 16-runner handicap hurdle which had been the cause of much study by Baxter. He had finally given it 'nightmare' status and was surprised to find a bookmaker hadn't sponsored it.

"Indeed I do" replied his aunt. "In fact, I've had 20p to win on it."

"Really" smiled Baxter "only I have the occasional flutter myself."

These words were the understatement of the century and equated to calling Hitler a trouble-maker. However, the old lady seemed more interested in eating her cake and Baxter went on in his preposterous vein.

"Naturally, I give any winnings to charity so if you let me know the name, you would be helping a very good cause."

"You're such a kind boy, William and I certainly want to assist you in such good work." She went over to the sideboard and produced an envelope. "I'll write down the name of the horse and put it inside here" she said.

Baxter smiled gratefully but as the main objective of his visit had already been spiked, there seemed little point in prolonging the company of his sweet but twittering aunt and her obnoxious parrot. He looked at his watch and said he had to get back to his office.

Once outside, he ripped open the envelope and read the name of the horse. What happened next was not the proposed dash to the nearest betting shop. Instead, his face adopted the look of a someone who has just discovered a dustbin in the middle of their front room. Baxter screwed up the piece of paper and tossed it away for the horse his aunt had given him was the only one he had confidently ruled out and, in his opinion, would finish 10 minutes behind the rest.

However, an hour later he was trying to kick himself in the pants for Aunt Ethel's tip had come in at 33-1. Baxter spent the rest of the day trying to convince himself that it was a fluke but the truth was that he was impressed and the thought of a missed 33-1 winner was as uncomfortable as a bout of indigestion.

The following morning, Baxter dug out his aunt's telephone number from the directory and rang her. After congratulating her on the tip, Baxter asked if she could possibly oblige with another, as there was a list of charities he wanted to donate to. His aunt was only too willing to help, asked him to wait five minutes and then returned with a horse in the 2 o'clock at Thirsk. Baxter thanked her and nipped down to the bank to cash another overdrawn cheque. From there he skipped back to his office to record the good news for his clients and to proof his selection to several sporting newspapers.

At ten minutes past two, Baxter left Armstrong's betting shop smiling broadly and padding out his wallet for Aunt Ethel's tip had just romped home at 6-1.

The next two days were hectic. Further calls to his aunt had produced two more lovely winners, new subscribers were coming in with every post and Baxter's screaming press advertisements were in type usually reserved for declarations of war.

Such was his success that Baxter began to speculate on what appeared to be a very prosperous future. If this kept up he would have to employ assistants and secretaries, new premises would have to be found, perhaps a whole new block to himself – as long as Aunt Ethel could keep producing the winners. But here a note of uncertainty crept into Baxter's thoughts. The whole operation was too haphazard. What would happen if his aunt's telephone went out of order? And could he tell his hundreds of eager clients that there was no selection today because Aunt Ethel had popped down to the supermarket to get a packet of osbornes or some seed for the despicable Peregrine?

Baxter decided that organisation was needed. He would have to find out his aunt's source of information and work directly with them. His aunt could be cut out with a consolatory box of chocolates – a large one, though, decided Baxter benevolently.

In fact, the box of chocolates wasn't all that large when he presented himself at his aunt's the next morning. Baxter could be quite charming when he made the effort and even retained his smile through a double rendering of "Hello, silly billy" from Peregrine. However, when Baxter tried to extract her source of information, the old lady was sweet but unhelpful.

"I really must keep that to myself" she said. "After all, we don't want these things getting about. It's really very unfair on the poor bookmakers."

Baxter considered this attitude combined sainthood and stupidity. His aunt left to make some tea in the kitchen while Baxter ground his teeth.

"I don't mind helping your charitable causes" she called "but I hope you didn't keep any of the money you won for yourself."

"Of course not" coughed Baxter.

"Yes, he did. Yes, he did" chimed the wretched parrot.

Baxter's frustration snapped and he took advantage of his aunt's absence to give the bird a sharp smack on the head with the box of chocolates. The bird toppled off its perch and hung dangling by the chrome chain around its leg before fluttering untidily back to its bar. The parrot still looked rather dazed when Baxter left.

Back home, Baxter decided that there was no point in worrying over his unsuccessful visit and that the main thing was that Aunt Ethel should continue passing on the information.

The next day was the Grand National. Could Aunt Ethel come up with the goods on the biggest betting day of the year? If she could then Baxter would feel justified in increasing the charge to his clients. After all, such red-hot information was priceless he told himself as he telephoned her number.

At last, his aunt answered the phone.

He rapped off a perfunctory "How are you, Auntie?" and almost in the same breath followed up with the request for the day's winner.

His aunt's reply stunned Baxter.

"What d'you mean, you can't give me a winner today?" he wailed. "It's Grand National day!"

"It's Peregrine, he's not himself today" said the aunt sadly.

"Peregrine?" repeated Baxter. "What's he got to do with it?"

"Well, I suppose you may as well know" she said quietly. "You see, every day I read Peregrine out the runners from the paper. He listens until eventually he'll interrupt me by saying 'That's a winner! That's a winner!' Unfortunately, today he said nothing. I think he may be sick."

The news that such a stupid bird as Peregrine could be the font of such racing wisdom, amazed Baxter. However, this was a crisis and action had to be taken.

"I'm coming over straightaway" he yelled into the phone.

Whether fresh grapes and vitamin tablets were suitable for sick parrots, Baxter wasn't sure but he bought some anyway. Sweeping past his aunt as she opened the door, he rushed forward to inspect the ailing avian.

"Hello silly billy" greeted the bird with only slightly less amusement.

"He seems all right to me" said Baxter ruefully and thinking the bird looked as perfectly horrid as usual.

"No, no, there's something wrong with him" persisted his aunt.

Baxter took out the grapes and began to feed the bird.

Peregrine disposed of them greedily until he had had enough at which point he ignored the next offering and, instead, gave Baxter a savage bite on the finger.

"He's still playful" said Aunt Ethel watching her nephew jump around like someone who has trod barefoot on an electric plug. With the pain eventually subsiding, Baxter recovered his demeanour and satisfied himself with a venomous glance at Peregrine.

"Let's try him with today's Grand National runners" ordered Baxter desperately.

His aunt picked up the paper and read each runner out slowly and distinctly. The list seemed to go on forever but the only sound from the bird was a yawn half-way through and, finally, a burp.

Baxter clenched his fists but remembered that his whole future depended on the well-being of Peregrine.

"You must get him to the vet this week-end. I know how important he is to you and we've got to do everything to get him well again. The cost doesn't matter" added Baxter, getting carried away.

"Oh, you're so kind, William, and I never thought you liked Peregrine."

Baxter left instructions that Peregrine take all the vitamin pills and that his aunt ring him first thing on Monday.

Baxter's face had the look of lost sleep on the Monday morning and he'd already smoked two consecutive cigarettes as he glared at the phone as though ready to pounce on it. At last, it sprang to life and he grabbed it.

"How is he?" shrieked Baxter.

"Oh, Peregrine's much better, thank you" said Aunt

Ethel "but I'm afraid he won't be able to give any more winners."

Her nephew's voice was almost hollow.

"No more winners?"

"I'm afraid not. You see when the vet examined him, he discovered a lump on Peregrine's head. It seems he bumped it in some way."

"Well, what if he did?" asked Baxter.

His aunt's reply made Baxter feel like burying the phone in his own head.

"It's made poor Peregrine deaf" she said.

PROOF OF INTELLIGENCE

For Baxter, the road to poverty was clear and open except for fellow travelers. Even these he seemed to pass with remarkable ease for there were no traffic lights and such was his speed that it seemed to be downhill all the way. Baxter didn't actually drive but in his mythical car there didn't appear to be any brake pedal in the shape of winners and if there was, Baxter couldn't find it. He would arrive there in no time at all and would probably set a course record. These were his thoughts as he contemplated another disastrous day's racing.

It was on these occasions that trivial things assumed great proportions and irritated him no end. Today, it had been when the TV paddock commentator had applied the phrase 'an intelligent head' to his fancy for the 2-year-old race.

Baxter could never understand it when horses were described in this way. He could concede that some had more attractive heads than others but how could you identify intelligence by appearance? Was it relevant anyway, they were athletes running a race and not sitting an exam? The only way Baxter would agree to the description was a head that went down on the line in front of all the others – now that was an intelligent head!

Sadly for Baxter, his fancy had moved with the speed of a rickshaw. If it did have any intelligence, he would have advised using it to open a horse-school teaching early entrance to the knacker's yard – the pass-rate would have been phenomenal. Had he not had a strong word for the 2 year-old, he may not have journeyed to Ripon at all as he'd always regarded it as a tricky course.

On the train back to London, he started to read his bedraggled copy of the Racing Post and came across the expression 'intelligent head' again in reference to another horse. Baxter simply wasn't having it! They were herd animals that by repetition and persuasion did what trainers taught them to do. Those that didn't, did not do so because of any reasoning on their part but simply because they lacked the ability or inclination. Besides, intelligence had no part in racing - "to the fastest, the prize" it was as simple as that. The way horses could manipulate his emotions confirmed a widely held belief that most horses were torment and frustration bagged in a leather skin.

It was a strange existence, spending his day in the pursuit of winners like a wild animal devotes itself in the search for food. His philosophic vein of thought continued. He doubted that there was any horseracing in Heaven and it seemed to Baxter that this was a wonderful incentive to lead a more Christian life and that if the Church preached along these lines instead of all the other guff, congregations would rocket. He thought of mentioning the idea to the local vicar when the train pulled into Kings Cross.

A little later, Baxter plodded up the stairs to his office and shut the door. He was immune to the jungle of disorder that surrounded him and had barely sat down when the phone rang.

"So you're back" said a voice.

"Yes" said Baxter recognising the clipped tones of Parr, a trainer in Royston who had a small string of jumpers.

"Any good?"

"Very bad" replied Baxter imitating the brevity.

"Never mind, one of mine will win tomorrow – Crazy Larry."

"He's next to useless."

"I know that's why *I've* got it. The others in the race are worse. Put your house on it!"

"I'd rather put your house on it" said Baxter recalling the horse's latest run.

"I want you to get me a thousand on at evens or better, anything above evens you can keep. Is that fair?"

"Certainly, let's hope it wins. Who's the jockey?"

"My son, Martin." There was only the sound of a disapproving grunt from Baxter. "I know you don't rate him but he's improving" went on the trainer.

Baxter felt there was as much chance of improvement as cellaring a £2.99 bottle of plonk. Although the lad claimed 7lb, it was Baxter's opinion that it should have been nearer twenty seven.

The race was at Fontwell, a course which didn't suit a lot of horses and another one which Baxter regarded as a tricky. By the following morning, he'd decided not to go but shortly before the race time he telephoned two of his credit accounts and had £500 with each at 11/10. However, the combination of bad horse and bad jockey was enough to dissuade him from any personal investment and he wandered down to Armstrong's shop with no great excitement. Up on the screens, the horses were lined up at the start and Crazy Larry's price was now evens. There were 6 runners and Baxter reckoned you could find better-looking horses in an abattoir.

After trailing the two leaders and surviving some shoddy

jumping, Crazy Larry moved up on the outside. One of the front two dropped away and after a bit of a ding-dong up the straight, the other horse turned it in and allowed Crazy Larry to win by a length. Missing a winner always rankled but Baxter consoled himself that in his present form, it probably wouldn't have won if he had have backed it and he'd earned himself £100, anyway.

Parr was on the phone later.

"Were we on?" he asked.

"You were" said Baxter. "I couldn't back it myself."

"Ran an intelligent race, didn't it."

The word was like a pinprick to Baxter.

"Intelligent?"

"Yes, didn't go charging off like it usually does – allowed my lad to hold him back."

"So now horses are intelligent!"

"They have a brain, don't they" offered Parr.

"And what's that got to do with intelligence?" countered Baxter. "All my clients have brains but if they had any sense they'd pack it in."

"True" said the trainer, a little too readily for Baxter's liking.

Baxter's outburst was ignorant and unlike him but he honestly couldn't recall any act of intelligence performed by a horse. However, his loss of form was clearly getting to him and the SureFire Tipping service made little progress over the following weeks and certainly nothing to justify paying Mrs Wilbow her rent. The subject was a minor concern to Baxter as he seldom paid it anyway but to his landlady it was a major concern because there was very little else going on in her life. Indeed, Baxter felt he was providing her therapy by giving her something to worry about

Although her concern grew with every unpaid week that passed, she would sometimes assume a detachment that was quite the opposite to what she felt inside and Baxter learnt to play this to his advantage. The signal for this gentle simmering beneath an air of tranquillity was when she started to hum. Mrs Wilbow often sang as she worked – to hum was quite different. Baxter would embrace the subject head on when the bee-like sounds penetrated his study of the racing press.

"I expect you're worried about the rent?" said Baxter.

"Not at all" said Mrs Wilbow "nothing was further from my mind." This was like an elephant denying an interest in buns.

Baxter seized the opportunity to close the subject.

"That's good, so long as you're not bothered. All in good time" he added and returned to his study of form.

Mrs Wilbow had been appeased, she'd made Baxter aware of the rent and she had seemed to behave magnanimously - the simple truth was, though, that Baxter still hadn't paid her.

It seemed that Parr had forgiven Baxter's belligerent mood for he rang him again.

"Just to tell you, The Yard is engaged at Kempton next week. He's fit enough to win first time out and you can back him with confidence."

This was indeed good news for The Yard was the only horse of any quality in Parr's stable. He was an 8-year-old gelding, a genuine 2-mile chaser who had won 12 races to date and had run up a sequence of five wins the previous season with Baxter on every time with increasing stakes. He had even contemplated sending the beast a gift-wrapped box of oats for Christmas – a plan that Baxter aborted when it got beat a neck trying to make it six. Still, there was no doubt that The Yard was a good sort and the news was like a light at the end of a tunnel.

"By the way" added Parr "you're wrong about intelligence and horses. The Yard is the smartest horse I've ever trained – I can even communicate with him!"

Baxter could feel himself bristling.

"Don't wind me up."

"It's true. Come down early to Kempton and I'll take you to the stables – you'll see."

Baxter's main concern on The Yard's seasonal debut was its likely price. Three's seemed the average forecast and Baxter thought that about right and was extremely bullish in advising it to his SureFire clients. However, so lamentable was his current form that if he predicted the sun would come up in the morning, most of them would have wanted at least 6/4.

Having arrived a couple of hours before racing, Baxter waited just inside the course entrance.

"Good to see you, Baxter. Follow me."

Parr led the way to the stables where a bay horse shifted restlessly in its box.

"He's on his toes. Can't wait to get out there" he said admiringly. He turned the horse's head towards them. "Now watch his mouth, Baxter." The trainer then addressed the horse. "Are you feeling good today?"

The horse pulled back its lips to reveal a formidable set of brown-streaked teeth.

"That means yes" explained Parr. Then again to the

horse. "Any problems at all?"

There was no re-action from the animal. "That's a no – nothing, see. Smart isn't he?"

"Never mind all that. Ask it if it's going to win" said Baxter getting agitated.

"He's a horse not a prophet, Baxter. He can't tell what's going to happen in a race. You expect too much but it's still intelligence in my book."

Baxter remained unconvinced. He was, however, impressed with The Yard in the race proper, as it came away from the last fence and slogged its way through the muddy conditions to overhaul the leaders. On faster ground, Baxter thought the result might have been different but he'd won a few bob and his tipping line had received a badly needed transfusion. He took a taxi back home from Waterloo and relished the winning feeling that erased past disappointments and made future ones tolerable.

It was a few weeks later that Baxter picked up the phone and recognised Parr's voice.

"What did you think of The Yard's last run?"

"Couldn't do no more than win but I thought it might have lost a bit of speed."

"Me, too. He's a bit older and becoming a bit of a lazy bugger. I'm thinking of running him over 3 miles at Wincanton. Similar track to Kempton – right-handed and flat. D'you think he'll stay?"

"Why don't you ask him?" said Baxter whose mouth was about to engulf a coffee-soaked rich tea finger before it disintegrated.

"Good idea" was followed by the sound of a chair scraping and retreating footsteps.

Baxter hadn't been serious in his suggestion and was beginning to regret his irony when Parr took so long it seemed liked he'd walked 3 miles to find out.

Eventually the trainer returned.

"He says yes. I'm still not sure but I think it's what he needs nowadays."

On the morning of the 3-miler at Wincanton, Baxter was in a quandary. The going was good as opposed to The Yard's previous run on soft but that didn't greatly bother Baxter and Marney, the jockey, certainly didn't - he was a top man and always rode the horse. No, the big doubt was the unknowable answer as to whether the horse stayed or not. In the end, Baxter decided to go with the horse. It was a good, genuine sort who didn't owe him a thing. Having made his decision, Baxter became extremely positive, put it out to his clients and took plenty of weaponry to bushwhack a few bookies. However, it wasn't a great card at Wincanton and a fair trip to boot so it was essential that The Yard obliged.

Before the race, Baxter joined Parr and the jockey in the parade ring. The trainer asked the horse if it felt good and the horse answered in the positive by pulling back its lips. After getting a leg-up, the jockey turned his mount towards the course while Baxter made hurried strides towards Tattersall's. Glancing at the boards, it was clear that the bookmakers were taking a pessimistic view of The Yard's first attempt at 3 miles and Baxter thought the 4 to 1 was a blinding price in a field of eight of which several others were trying the trip for the first time. He managed to get all his bet on at 4's plus a couple of hundred for Parr before it was cut in to 7-2. The next 7 minutes was a time of sublime pleasure for Baxter as The Yard went round jumping from fence to fence, ears pricked

"The horse pulled back its lips"

and never touching a twig. After the first circuit, it was 10 lengths ahead and the final winning margin was a distance.

"Never backed an easier winner" was how Baxter summed it up.

"The good news is that he's entered in another 3-miler here next week" smiled Parr. "Of course, he'll carry a penalty."

"Never mind that" replied Baxter "they'll need a sledgehammer to stop him winning." He gave a complimentary rub to the horse's nose and sauntered off to collect from some unwelcoming faces in the ring.

The re-appearance of The Yard was awaited impatiently by Baxter for since the Wincanton success he had made a sizeable dent in his winnings by backing a couple of *stumers* that had jumped with all the agility of a lobster. It seemed The Yard was the only horse he could trust. At least, it knew how to win so in that sense he was intelligent even if the communicating with Parr was a bit hard to swallow.

The obvious snag to The Yard's appearing to be a good thing on the Wincanton card was that the price was going to be skinny. Baxter clients didn't like skinny prices even when they won so there was nothing to be gained from putting it out. A 'no selection' message was therefore left on his tipping line while its proprietor planned a sizeable investment on what he deemed a racing certainty so long as The Yard jumped the 21 fences.

On the train to the course, Baxter looked across the Somerset countryside where a line of lime trees stripped by the October winds of their leaves stood naked like windjammers in dock. Baxter didn't know exactly what a windjammer was but he knew that's what he was reminded of.

"Feeling good, everything okay?" said Parr looking at The Yard.

The horse bared its teeth as Baxter looked on.

"Same as last time, eh?" the trainer added.

Baxter noted The Yard didn't re-act to this question but the trainer didn't appear to notice and slapped the horse's neck.

"He's a good sort – wish I had another like him. Getting a bit smart now though. I'd only have to open his stable door before and he'd trot out to be tacked up for his morning work – now I have to lead him out."

"So long as he saves his energy for the track" said Baxter. "You backing him?"

"I'll have a monkey at 2's on or better otherwise I'll settle for the prize money."

Baxter regarded The Yard's price in the ring with dismay. Okay, so there were only 4 runners in a same grade race as it had won so easily a week earlier but there were still two circuits to complete. Even certainty had a price in Baxter's book and it seemed he was not going to have a bet at all until one bookmaker chalked up 2/5 just to take a bet and Baxter stepped in with £600. He was still deliberating on the wisdom of this when it went to 2/7 and made him feel that perhaps he'd done the right thing. In fact, he hadn't.

Marney jumped The Yard to the front from the start but after turning into the back straight, the second favourite joined him and they jumped round together. Of the pair, The Yard seemed to be going the better and his jumping was certainly cleaner. Despite this, Baxter was never as relaxed as on the previous run. This time he had a nagging sense of doom and it happened very suddenly soon after the last fence in front of the stands. The Yard had gone a length up and started to look around, Marney gave it a slap but it continued to turn its head to both sides before slowing abruptly to a trot. Marney kicked and slapped and cursed but The Yard would have none of it. The other horses had all gone on and it was a bit pointless for Marney to give the horse another crack. The Yard resented the abuse, reared up and deposited his jockey on the ground before trotting off towards the paddock. Baxter was dismayed rather than angry. Something had gone wrong, he'd sensed it happening but couldn't explain it. He joined Parr and a furious-looking Marney in the unsaddling enclosure. Marney used up a few expletives before the word 'idiot' and limped off towards the weighing room.

"Strange thing is, that's exactly what The Yard isn't" said Parr.

"But why did he pull himself up?" asked Baxter. "He seems sound enough."

"Like I've said, The Yard is an intelligent animal" said Parr patting the horse's neck.

"Yes, you keep telling me that" said Baxter wryly.

"Add in the fact he's getting lazy and I reckon he remembered his first run over 3 miles round here. See, once he passed the post after the first circuit he saw little point in running round again to end up where he already was." The horse's head was between the two men. Parr turned to the horse. "Isn't that right, you rascal?"

Baxter looked at the horse's mouth and saw it move. This time he knew it was a grin.

BEATING THE COMPETITION

There was nothing quite like winning. The joy of being right, the comforting warmth of taking other people's money and the exhilarating surge that revitalised you in the knowledge that the gods had smiled on you at last. Of course, this feeling was one that Baxter was recalling from memory because at the present moment he was doing his brains. So, it was perverse that he should be thinking in such a way. Perhaps he was reminiscing because it was never to return and had passed into history – well, that's what it felt like.

The strange working of Baxter's mind was often of some concern to him. Why it had ever come to the conclusion earlier in the day that Cinnamon Wage could win the 3.0'clock race at Thirsk was a prime example. A horse with the battling qualities of an Italian infantryman, ridden by a jockey that would give a bike a bad back and trained by a man who couldn't train a seal to eat fish. And yet Baxter had been sucked in. Of course, there were mitigating circumstances – Baxter had watched the horse make late headway over 5 furlongs in its previous race and it was now racing over 6 furlongs. It had also travelled over 250 miles to be there and was in a seller for the first time but it was the greed invoked by the 10 to 1 on the boards that really blew his reservations away. It looked big to Baxter and when it went down to 4 to1 at the off, it looked absolutely massive. Unfortunately, beating the odds was not the same as winning and Cinnamon Wage got worried out of it in the last half furlong and was beaten a neck. Baxter had great difficulty in refraining from asking the person nearest him to give him a good kick up the backside.

Instead he thrust his head into his racing paper and looked to redeem himself. However, it was not to be and he backed two more losers. As he made his way out towards the station, he was quite oblivious to the picturesque backdrop of the Hambleton Hills and the attractiveness of the North Yorkshire track and he could only focus on his disappointment.

The train journey back to Kings Cross gave him plenty of time for thought to a recurring problem with the SureFire Tipping Service. It was the same for every tipping service and every gambling operator – the need for new clients. Shrinkage of current accounts was inevitable – many became disillusioned, some indeed ended up with no boots, moved away or even died. They had to be replaced and, although success provided the greatest boost, it could never be sustained. Advertising helped but was expensive and outside Baxter's budget at the moment. In fact, most things were outside Baxter's budget at this moment.

It was difficult to find adults who still believed in fairy tales because that was exactly what Baxter was peddling. He was putting himself up as some sort of wizard who could forecast the outcome of races - despite all its vagaries - and make the believers rich. The delusion was so attractive that people willingly paid to discover what inherently they already knew – that it was impossible. Yes, human nature was a wonderful thing conceded Baxter. If only he could find a few more people like Hugo Simpson who had been with him since the very beginning and who still regarded Baxter as brilliant despite this not being verified by reality.

Hugo was a wonderful, cheery person with a permanent smile that some people found disconcerting, particularly those visiting his undertaking premises.

Baxter bumped into him occasionally at southern tracks and this was the case when he went to the Windsor meeting on the following Monday.

"Baxter, have you seen this?" he said waving a flyer excitedly.

"Of course, they're giving them out all over the place – I dumped mine" replied Baxter.

"Dumped it!" echoed Hugo "Why it's a doddle – even I can answer the questions. You can win a million!"

Baxter had read the flyer thrust into his hand by a pretty girl but had treated it with the disdain it deserved. There were 5 questions to answer in a multiple-choice form but Baxter never read beyond the first, which was: Who was the jockey of the 1986 Derby winner, The Minstrel?

Was it (a) Lester Piggott
(b) Monty Python
(c) The Dalai Lama

It was an insult to any racegoer's intelligence although he'd already heard someone voice the opinion that this was a trick question and that the answer was, in fact, Monty Python who had been a late jockey change.

"Look, Hugo, everyone's going to get the answers right – d'you think you're all going to win a million?" said Baxter. "Use your loaf!"

"Well, that what it says" said Hugo pointing to the flyer.

Hugo was about as sharp as a marble - a fact that was

"People found his smile disconcerting"

reinforced in Baxter's opinion by the knowledge that the undertaker had been married four times.

"By the way, I got married again since I last saw you" said Hugo as if he'd just changed his car.

Baxter said nothing but just gazed at the man in sympathy.

"Retired school teacher and loves coming racing with me. Bit of a shrewdy with figures she is because that was her subject see – maths" went on Hugo. "She looks at the odds and can tell me the percentages and when the prices should get bigger. And if she thinks a horse's price is too short she won't let me back it no matter how much I fancy it." He laughed – a rather empty laugh. "D'you know I used to back three or four in the same race sometimes. Can't do that now – she won't let me. She says it's a fool's way to bet! Yes, she's definitely saving me money." He paused and added wistfully "Trouble is, I don't enjoy it so much."

Baxter understood. It wasn't that Hugo liked losing but he did accept it as part of the expense for enjoying himself. As a bachelor, Baxter thought the new discipline imposed on Hugo was both unacceptable and regrettable but he could hardly tell him so. Instead he tried to offer some crumb of comfort.

"She probably thinks she's helping and besides it doesn't do any harm to cut out some of the deadwood in your betting."

"I'm glad you feel like that Baxter because she's told me to cancel my subscription to your tipping service" announced Hugo.

"What! After all these years?" whined Baxter in a voice of someone who has just had something heavy dropped on their foot.

"Yes, she analysed your tips over the last 6 months and reckons a monkey with a pin would have done better."

"Oh, did she?" said Baxter, wounded by the comparison and aggrieved that this reformation of Hugo was to hurt him financially.

From about 100 yards away he noticed a woman waving her arm as she approached in their direction. Even from this distance he could she was a stoutly built woman and striding towards them with some purpose.

"Here she comes now" said Hugo of his wife. "Would you like to meet her?"

Baxter had the look of a 1903 bookmaker who had laid Hackler's Pride to the hilt in the Cambridgeshire and was watching it doddle up. As she approached, he could see a fiercely determined face and an introduction that held all the attraction of a free haircut at Sweeney Todd's.

"Not just now, Hugo" said Baxter hastily "especially after slurring my reputation." He moved away.

"I'm sorry, Baxter – she's like the Iron Chancellor with my money."

Having lost his most loyal supporter, Baxter was badly in need of a boost to his confidence. He was hoping this would be provided by a 3-year-old colt which was running in the second race and which he had put on his tipping line. Unfortunately, the animal had run with the speed of a crowned turkey and was either totally unsuited by the firm conditions or was wise beyond its years and clearly intent on saving its energy for stud duties.

In contrast to the Windsor going, Baxter's life was run in permanently searching conditions – the quest for winners and new clients and the danger of impending poverty saw to that. The proximity of the latter state was underlined the following morning when he opened his bank statement. The financial status of his bank account could only occasionally have been considered the stuff of which oaks were made but right now it looked as if a lumberjack had attacked it.

Baxter grimaced. A transfusion was needed but he was out of form and his current information was as reliable as a railway timetable. Of course, he could take a chance and slam into a short priced favourite on one of his credit accounts but he knew it was well-worn path to Carey Street. No, the risk-free solution was new clients – the believers of dreams. He knew there were out there but how could he find them without the expense of advertising? It wasn't as if you could look them up in Yellow Pages under 'mugs'. It was a problem that was to become more acute in the following weeks as his luck remained at its low ebb and his expenses mounted.

Then suddenly the dawn of opportunity appeared in the Racing Post. Baxter had clean forgotten the business of the 'Win a Million' competition but the truth of it had now emerged. Because the entry was free it wasn't apparent at first that it was a scam and the winners - which included nearly everyone - were duly notified of their good fortune in becoming millionaires. However, to claim the money the winners had to send a £100 administration fee to the organisers. Of course, it couldn't be genuine but the fear of missing out on becoming a millionaire for the sake of £100 was a haunting prospect to many and besides they had answered the questions correctly they told themselves.

The result was that hundreds of people had sent of

their administration fee and were still waiting for their million pound cheque that never arrived and never would. The police had now been brought in to collect evidence for a prosecution and the Thames Valley Police were holding a meeting to which anyone who had been a victim of the scam were urged to attend.

This was more than Baxter could have hoped. An assembly of gilt-edged fools were to meet in Reading the following Thursday evening. What an opportunity! All Baxter had to do was obtain their names and addresses and offer them the services of the SureFire Tippng Service. He would probably wait a little while they got over their latest setback but what a treasure trove he would have in store.

By the date of the meeting, Baxter had formulated his simple plan and arrived very early at the hall. He had brought with him a folding chair and table and positioned himself inside the entrance. He then put a sheet of paper and a clipboard in front of him and wrote out a sign marked 'RECEPTION' which he taped to the front of the table.

Soon, people started to drift in. Baxter greeted them cheerfully and asked them to sign in sometimes adding 'damn shabby trick' or 'we only enter these competitions for a bit of fun' as a sort of comfort. Nobody seemed to mind giving their details and when a police inspector arrived he merely nodded at Baxter before going into the hall.

Baxter was looking at his list with great satisfaction when Hugo Simpson entered.

"Well, well, if it isn't Baxter" he said smiling. "I thought you weren't having anything to do with this business."

"And I didn't "explained Baxter. "Just helping out."

"You were right, too good to be true, wasn't it? I would

have fallen for it too, if it hadn't been for the wife."

"But I thought you did enter the competition. Isn't that why you're here?" asked Baxter.

"Yes, I did and when they told me I'd won, I was all for sending off the £100 but the wife wasn't having it. I begged her to let me because there was just the possibility that there was a million pound cheque waiting for me."

"So what happened?"

"Well, I think I mentioned that she was a shrewdy and she came up with this brilliant idea."

From the hall, Baxter could hear that the meeting was about to start and folded up his chair and table.

"And what exactly was that, Hugo?"

"Well, she wrote them a note saying take the £100 from the million I'd won and send me the balance!"

Baxter smiled as he took the sheet from the clipboard and folded it carefully into his inside pocket.

"You had a result there, Hugo - and so have I!"

ON A DIFFERENT LEVEL

It was Bath's first July meeting and the 5-furlong sprint handicap of 19 runners was a Grade A headscratcher specifically designed to plump up bookmakers' satchels and rack up admissions to sanatoriums for the confused and brain-addled.

As a professional, Baxter recognised it for the minefield it was but on this occasion the name of Lookinforgolfballs stood out as if written in illuminated manuscript. The truth was that Baxter had broken one of his cardinal rules of never falling in love with a horse. Lookinforgolfballs was a four-year-old black filly that he had followed since her two-year-old debut at Brighton. Tall, sleek, wonderful head and clear eye she could run a bit too and she'd gone into Baxter's notebook as a certain future winner. Unfortunately, like many of the horses in the book, Lookinforgolfballs was finding it difficult to fulfil this prediction and whereas all other duds were quickly scorched from its pages with merciless venom, the filly was allowed to remain. It was becoming a costly residence because she had now run six times, had never won and been placed only twice. Despite this, Baxter continued to find excuses for her –'wrong going', 'badly drawn', 'poor jockey', and 'unlucky in running' but always omitted 'slow'.

However, she had been running in good company and being convinced there was a decent race in her, Baxter wanted to be on when it happened. She was near the top of the handicap and was only 10 to 1, which didn't seem great odds for a lottery but Baxter stuck a fifty on her anyway. His printed ticket seemed fragile in comparison to the old style coloured betting card and not half as satisfying if the horse it represented got beat. At least, you could give the old tickets a good pummelling, strangle them into some sort of ball and give them a hefty kick into space. The flimsy replacements just weren't up to allowing such a healthy release of emotion.

Baxter was now standing close to where the horses were coming out on to the course and thought how well the filly looked when he glanced a movement to his side and saw a thick black line being drawn through Lookinforgolfballs on the race-card. His offended gaze looked up to the tall scribbler, who had a small nose and large eyes set in a wide, round face and resembled a tawny owl.

"D'you know something, I don't?" asked Baxter indicating the line through Lookinforgolfballs.

"Only that it's extremely unlikely to win" said the man with an assured grin.

"I've backed it" asserted Baxter "I follow the horse."

"Me, too, but it won't win at this level."

"It's a tough handicap alright" agreed Baxter, slightly put out by the authorative tone of the man. "You sound like a real racing man?"

"Yes, I'm in the field of equine research."

"Oh yes" replied Baxter with the voice of a man who thought he knew what it involved but realised he didn't have a clue.

"I'm working on the SARP project – you may have heard about it."

"I think I may have" pretended Baxter, not wanting to

appear entirely ignorant but fearing the man had already reached this conclusion.

"Pity you backed Lookinforgolfballs though – almost certainly done your money."

He smiled at Baxter, doffed his hat and walked off. Lookinforgolfballs didn't win. Her performance could have been read as disappointing or promising depending on your view of the filly. Baxter summed it up as 'behind early, late progress, one paced' but was still convinced she had a decent race in her.

Baxter didn't have another bet that afternoon and his only consolation was the note of the runner-up in the last race whose jockey sat like a sack of potatoes for most of the race and was still only beaten half a length. Its name went into his 'Horses to Follow' notebook which, while having had its successes, could have been more suitably re-titled as 'A Guide to Disposable Wealth'. Its use was for Baxter's own personal betting whereas his SureFire Tipping Service mainly ran on stable information and racing contacts.

As he'd left a 'No Selection Today' message on the service it meant there was no emotion of either elation or despair and also gave the illusion that the selections were carefully screened and distilled before being offered to clients. On the other hand, it did create the mystery of why so many got beat and why the success rate was hugely inferior to Ethel's, who worked in the local fish and chip shop, didn't know where a saddle went and won six grand on a super yankee in Armstrong's betting shop.

Of course, the answer was luck – that elusive intangible commodity which changed lives, made rich men fools and fools rich men. There were times when Baxter felt he was

"It's name went into his 'Horses to Follow' notebook"

destined never to be rich and was foolish to even try but the challenge kept him going. Indeed, he was already looking at tomorrow's runners as his train pulled into Kings Cross.

He took a taxi to his office, climbed the stairs and sat back in his chair. From the drawer he took a bottle of Macallan and poured himself a glass. The liquid tingled in his mouth and he remembered the man in equine research. He even remembered the acronym SARP and wondered what it stood for. Then he stopped remembering anything and fell asleep.

It wasn't until the following month that Baxter found Lookinforgolfballs entered up again. It was due to run at Goodwood and it seemed that connections had given up any aspirations for the filly as it was entered in a seller. Baxter studied the race and concluded that despite a large field, most of the runners were as slow as treacle and that Lookinforgolfballs had a great chance. Baxter made up his mind to have a good crack on her so he was rather inconvenienced when a highly-regarded contact rang him with the information that another horse in the same race was 'the one to be on'.

It sometimes happened that stable tips were quite unjustified to Baxter's reading of the formbook but he was always willing to change his mind especially as he wasn't privy to the shenanigans and plots of the trainers to whom conspiracy was an art form.

So, on the morning of the race, Bulletproof Tie was put forward to his clients whereas Baxter went to Goodwood with his intention of backing Lookinforgolfballs still intact. The crowd was unusually small for Goodwood and it wasn't long before he spotted the owl-like face of the man he'd seen at Bath. Baxter noted that the man divided his time between the paddock area and watching the races and with little interest in the bookmakers.

When Lookinforgolfballs was due to run, Baxter went over to the parade ring to see how she looked. To his eye she looked particularly well whereas the informant's tip had a coat like matt paint and the undefined head of a block of wood. The man from equine research was also there and Baxter could see that once again a bold black line had been scored through the name of Lookinforgolfballs on the man's race card.

"Got a great chance today – she's better than selling class" said Baxter as the horse came round in front of them.

The man looked across and his owlish face broke into a smile.

"Hello". He paused. "I agree with you but I still can't see her winning – this isn't the right course for her."

This didn't put off Baxter because racing was all about opinions but the man did seem to have a reserve of reasons as to why Lookinforgolfballs wouldn't win.

"D'you like Bulletproof Tie?" said Baxter.

"I do actually" said the man surprised. "My research suggests it will run well here. Are you backing it?"

"No" smiled Baxter perversely "I'm backing Lookinforgolfballs" and strolled off unaware that the man was shaking his head in dismay.

Moments after the race, Baxter was doing exactly the same thing. Lookinforgolfballs had always been up there but had run fifth without ever looking like winning. He did feel a little better when the result of the photo finish was announced because Bulletproof Tie had got up on the line at

6 to 1 and his clients would no doubt be temporarily impressed. The fact that Baxter hadn't fancied it, hadn't backed and had, indeed, opposed it would have confused them in much the same way as Baxter confused himself. It was the sort of torment that Baxter regularly imposed upon himself and was part of the agony of betting horses.

The success of Bulletproof Tie heralded a slump in the fortunes of the SureFire Betting Service and its only subsequent winner was a 3's on chance who dead-heated, had to survive an objection and whose jockey was fined for over-use of the whip. It was with little enthusiasm then that he received reports from contacts and with growing reluctance that he posted off their monthly retainers. Racing though was in full flow for it was June and holiday crowds were swelling racecourse attendances. Again the name of Lookinforgolfballs loomed out to him from the newspaper but by now Baxter was out of love with the filly. She had cost him dear and had been finally removed from his note- book.

He also noted that the race she was in at Sandown Park was a Listed Race and, on all known form, was clearly out of her depth. In fact, her forecast odds of 33-1 seemed cramped to Baxter and he wondered why she'd been entered at all.

However, it was a good card, the track was easy to get to for Baxter and he was looking forward to going. On the journey to Sandown, Baxter felt a certain unease for while it seemed distinctly unlikely that Lookinforgolfballs could win against quality horses, there was always the possibility that Sod's law would operate and the very time he let her go unbacked, she would win. This thought was very much in his mind as he watched her in the parade ring. As always, she looked well and was to be ridden by a 7lb claiming apprentice who Baxter considered on the over-rated side of useless. Being a Listed race the youngster was unable to claim his allowance so it didn't seem the brightest of moves on the part of his connections. This time it was owl-face who spotted Baxter.

"Hello, I thought I'd find you here."

"Don't worry, I'm not backing Lookinforgolfballs – I've given up on her" said Baxter.

"You can't do that" said the man earnestly "this is what she's been waiting for. I ran into her trainer after the last run at Goodwood and gave him my advice. He didn't seem convinced but maybe that's why she's here today."

"Well, if she couldn't win that seller what chance can she have in this Listed Race?" asked Baxter.

"Quite different today" the man from equine research said firmly.

"She's 40's on the book."

"Good heavens that's ridiculous! Look, I rarely bet but put £10 on her for me" said the man reaching for his wallet.

Baxter took the tenner and went off to the ring and put it on. The bookie rubbed the price off but it was still widely available. Baxter paused for a moment before putting on another tenner for himself. He couldn't help it and what was a tenner, after all?

Lookinforgolfballs was clipped in to 25's at the off so at least he'd nicked the price which was often the same sort of comfort you got when you paid £200 less than the asking price for a Cartier wrist watch only to find that it's a forgery anyway.

As the stalls opened, the filly shot into the lead with the

apprentice either unwilling or unable to hold her back. It wasn't something Baxter could recall her doing before and she blazed along with the other runners idling along behind and giving her a soft lead. However coming into the home turn, the other jockeys were showing some concern and started to get to work. They pushed, they urged, they wielded their bats as they closed on the filly who was doing no more than keeping up her gallop. The distance between her nearest pursuer was shrinking, ever shrinking, but it was too late and Lookinforgolfballs held on by a neck. Yards past the post she was passed by two horses and there was a loud criticism that the other jocks had ridden a terrible race.

Baxter, in his state of delirium was unaware of such criticism.

"Made all – brilliant!" was his post-race summing up as he embraced the tall, restrained figure from equine research.

With a smile so wide as to reveal dentistry to his back teeth, he went off to collect.

On a table in the bar, Baxter's companion had laid out several charts and was still looking rather studious.

"It's so nice when your theories work out in practice" he said.

Baxter, already on his third glass, looked at them with a gaze that was becoming extremely unfocused and spoke in a voice that was slurred and dull.

"So you're saying that Lookinforgolfballs couldn't win at Bath or Goodwood because she was racing at the wrong altitude."

"For her, it was. Those two courses are amongst the highest in Britain – here at Sandown Park she was racing at one of the lowest and that suited her. You see, that's what the

SARP project is – the Study of Altitude on Racehorse Performance. It seems that altitude levels affect horses in different ways. Before today, Lookinforgolfballs had raced at the wrong level."

Baxter was more of the opinion that the apprentice had been carted off in the race but this was a time to enjoy, a time for harmony.

"Well" said Baxter "so it's another statistic to take into account when studying form?"

"Yes" said the man "the publication of the study well may initiate this."

Baxter smiled and looked fondly at the amber liquid in his glass. Bathed in it he could see the image of the filly just holding on at the line. She'd repaid his trust and his judgement.

"Well, it doesn't matter how you find them" he conceded " but weren't we lucky and wasn't it great!"

NO SENTIMENT IN RACING

Baxter was enjoying one of those rare exhilarating periods in his disheartening existence as a racehorse tipster and was giving his bookmakers the sort of hammering usually confined to blacksmith's workshops. This oasis in what was usually a desert of despair had come about because, quite simply, he had struck form. The week so far had produced no less than five winners and the effect it had on Baxter's life was profound. New subscriptions trickled happily into his mail either from recommendation or from the trumpeting adverts he placed in the sporting press. In addition, his recently installed premium phone line gave promise of being an additional buoy in keeping the SureFire Tipping Service afloat.

Regular trips to the bank to pay in cheques were a pleasure Baxter had almost forgotten and he no longer viewed trainers, jockeys and bookies with the acrimonious thoughts that had previously sprung so readily to mind.

Although thoughts of women seldom pierced the cloistered world of Baxter's life, he even reserved a kindly thought for Mrs Wilbow so that when she came to collect his rent he greeted her warmly. This unnerved her considerably and she was further stunned when she actually got paid. Crisp £10 notes were peeled off from a fat bundle and handed over with abandon. She left, promising to pinch herself later. She also considered buying some carpet for the wooden stairs but decided the occasion momentous enough to disregard such a mundane purchase and went for a new hat instead.

Yes, life was good, reflected Baxter looking out of his office window with the benign smile of a vicar counting the collection tray after the Christmas service. Even the rain bucketing down couldn't subdue the humane glow that radiated from his heart. Indeed, it only intensified it for had he not received information from his Newmarket source that Criminal Custard in the 4.0 race was a confirmed mud lark and would oblige comfortably. Such information would normally have merited a tilt at the bookies on the course but the thought of a trip to Huntingdon held little appeal and the rest of the card was so poor that he doubted the value of seeing such a lot of discredited animals attempt to run. Instead, he decided to make one of his rare visits to the local betting shop.

Having recorded his subscriber's message urging maximum support for Criminal Custard, Baxter spent a pleasant lunchtime in the pub. His new-found bonhomie even extended to buying the new barman a couple of drinks - an unrewarding gesture when it transpired that the man 'had no interest in horses or tips'.

From there he went to Armstrong's betting shop, a shabby, quiet establishment which, judging by the notices on the wall, had more limits than the statute book. Baxter wrote out £200 to win on Criminal Custard and handed the bet to the cashier. This caused as much consternation as if he'd written out 'THIS IS A HOLD-UP'. The startled woman hurried out to the back-room, there was some animated conversation, a chair scraped a floor and finally Armstrong appeared.

"Oh, it's you, Baxter. Thought it might be someone who knew something."

Baxter smiled, his serenity undiminished by the remark, and watched Armstrong ring the bet up with a degree of relish. As he was leaving, he noticed Old Harry sitting on a stool in the corner. Old Harry was an inveterate punter and even at this early stage of the afternoon, there were enough crumpled betting slips beneath his feet to send a park-keeper into a frenzy. Baxter went over to him.

"How's your luck, Harry?"

Years of unsuccessful punting had etched form lines of despair on the grey face that turned around.

"All bad - same as ever." Then suddenly the sad eyes sparkled and a crinkled smile generated affection. "Still, Ada Rose is going in the last - get me out of trouble she will."

Baxter screwed his face in dismay. Ada Rose was probably the most worthless animal ever to step on a racecourse, a rogue without a doubt, still a maiden at seven and with as much speed as a pack mule. Of course, Old Harry was not such a mug as to be unaware of these deficiencies but Ada Rose also happened to be the name of his wife.

From what Baxter heard, the other Ada Rose was as undesirable as the horse. Many years before she had run off with a tally man and left Harry to bring up three kids without so much as a subsequent postcard. However, the fatal voice of sentiment still echoed in Harry's brain and her namesake carried his money whenever it ran - which had been often and abysmally.

"Listen, forget about Ada Rose" advised Baxter earnestly "it couldn't win a race against Long John Silver!" He lowered

"Old Harry was an inveterate punter"

his voice. "I'm going to do you a favour, Harry. You know I get information from time to time and just now the information is red hot. My clients pay good money for this stuff but I'll tell you this one for free." Old Harry was nodding his head. "Criminal Custard in the 4.0 clock is a good thing. Put on as much as you can afford and you can thank me very much after." He slipped the old man a fiver.

"Ta, Mr Baxter. I looked at that one - got a bit of a chance, I reckon" said Old Harry.

Baxter was less than delighted by Old Harry's testimony to the horse's chance and at any other time it may have been cause for reconsideration. However, right now Baxter felt supreme.

"Don't tell anyone else and help yourself to it. Forget all the other horses today and especially forget Ada Rose" ended Baxter. He left the shop with a warmth known only to the greatest benefactors.

"Whe-e-e!" exclaimed Baxter joyfully as he put down the phone.

It was shortly after 4 p.m. and he had just heard that Criminal Custard had gone in at 3-1 which meant a personal profit of £600 not to mention the salutary effect this latest success would have on his business. He lit a small cigar and poured himself a large Macallan. Winning was a great feeling and, for Baxter, unsurpassable.

The rain had now stopped. Baxter checked that the winning receipt was in his wallet and left for Armstrong's betting shop. Like remnants of a defeated army, a small flow of punters was leaving as he arrived. Racing was over, the littered floor about to be swept by the cashier who was now doubling as the cleaner.

Armstrong was grim-faced and silent as he paid out the cash. Baxter smiled but made no quip to Armstrong. His equanimity put him above such baseness and although he'd only had one, he felt beautifully drunk.

As he stuffed the money into his wallet, he saw Old Harry still sitting in the corner by the door.

"Well, what did I tell you?" grinned Baxter.

The old fellow nodded and there was an attempt at a smile but he didn't quite make it. "Oh yeah, good one that."

The voice was joyless and carried a certain lack of gratitude that troubled Baxter. "You did back it didn't you?" he asked.

"Course I did" said Old Harry glumly.

"Thank goodness for that then" said Baxter. He looked directly into the eyes. They were sad and watery. "Is anything the matter?"

Old Harry unfolded a betting slip and looked at it. "Did it in a double with Ada Rose, didn't I?"

A MAJOR MEETING

A trace of despair was leaking into the air of the office of the SureFire Tipping Service and Baxter's dream of success was as far away as ever. Indeed, he wondered why he even contemplated he could beat the supreme enemy to the extent that he could retire and go racing just for fun. Yet it had to be possible. After all, amongst every list of runners was the eventual winner and all you had to do was find it. Difficult, of course, but it wasn't like trying to climb Mount Everest with hiking boots, a knapsack and a bar of Kendal mint. Compared to that, winner finding should have been a doddle. It was this optimism that was Baxter's lifeblood. The pulse was so low at times that it seemed expiry was imminent but it never failed to revive. Tomorrow was another day, Life had to go on, disasters overcome.

Occasionally he wondered if he should give the game up altogether but the truth was that he was a man of fifty and quite unqualified for absolutely everything. All he knew was racing, all he cared about was racing – he couldn't give the game up if he tried. Why only that morning he had given another confident selection on his tipping line, the subscribers to which were fast becoming an endangered species.

He checked the Lester Piggott wall-clock and rang his bookmaker to see how it had got on. There was a pause, a slight unease, then relief – Burning Daylight had triumphed at 2-1 on. Okay, so it wasn't an exactly brilliant selection but there were plenty of 2's on chances that got beat. At once, despair had been swept from the room. – he was feeling good again.

It was very much the same frame of mind that saw him at Charing Cross station the following morning. The station was buzzing with Bank Holiday travellers and he was on his way to Epsom. His study of the form book the previous evening had gone on well into the night but he reckoned he'd dug up a couple of good things which might just ransack a few hods.

Engrossed in his sporting paper, Baxter took only a sub-conscious interest in the train's progress. He knew the stops to Epsom like the back of his hand and it was only when pulling away from a second unfamiliar station that he wailed out.

"I'm on the wrong train! I should be going to Epsom."

There were a few smothered smiles from those around him but, otherwise, Baxter's announcement was met with general unconcern. Apart that is from an elderly man, with a florid face and friendly brown button eyes, seated on the opposite side of the carriage. He was wearing a County Set ensemble of Tattersall check shirt, silk tie, green tweed jacket, brown moleskin trousers and brown brogue shoes.

Baxter was now on his feet and extremely agitated about being trapped in a train going in the wrong direction. The other man, levered himself up with the aid of a cane and came across whereupon it became evident that he was carrying enough weight to stop a Group One winner in a seller.

"This is the race-train to Folkestone" said the man. "I

"His study of the form book had gone on well into the night"

should stay on – I'm going there myself."

"But I've got a couple of good things for Epsom" complained Baxter.

"Don't bother with them – I have information for Folkestone that comes direct from the trainers. I'll share it with you if you'll come along."

Baxter did a mental about turn. He wasn't going to get to Epsom in time, he could still get a bet on though and perhaps also clean up at Folkestone with Major Theakstone, formerly of the Coldstream Guards, for this was how the man identified himself.

Folkestone was not a racecourse that Baxter relished. It was a place that always seemed to get cold and even with the sun streaming down there was a bite in the air. However, the Major was a cheery old cove and told Baxter he came to this meeting every year. Several bookmakers obviously knew him and greeted him with smiles and even laughter.

Baxter was studying the first race when the Major wobbled off on his cane to a rails bookmaker. He said nothing on his return except "We'll see what happens here."

This seemed a welcome precaution to Baxter – after all, the information had to be tested. As two horses flashed past the post locked together, it was obvious the photo finish was going to be tight.

Major Theakstone seemed unperturbed. "I've backed a winner" he said, moving off.

"But it's a photo" called Baxter after the pottering figure.

The remark was met with a dismissive wave from the Major's free hand. He returned a little later after the result was announced.

"Five hundred quid on that" he said. "How much do I win?"

"Well, it's returned at 7 to 1, so that's three and a half grand" replied Baxter, alarmed at the Major's lack of simple arithmetic and even more surprised that he'd been able to get such a sizeable bet on at a place like Folkestone.

"Of course, I bet on the rails on my credit account – I don't have the cash. Fancy a drink?"

Sitting in the bar, Baxter had an increasing liking for the Major with much of it influenced by his access to apparently sound information.

"That was a nice touch" congratulated Baxter.

"Oh, I do it all the time. Of course, I don't get out much because I'm not really a well man but I bet on the phone rather a lot."

"So any tip for the next race?" said Baxter.

"Tip?" queried the Major.

"Yes, information" said Baxter, slightly disappointed that he'd not been told the first winner.

The Major looked blankly at the card, frowned and shook his head.

Baxter began to notice that the Major operated in either a mode of extreme animation or one of sublime tranquillity and although the change could be quite sudden it was always signalled by the dilation of his eyes.

"So" he said, suddenly brightening up with a chuckle "tell me about yourself, Baxter."

Baxter felt a bit uncomfortable about the request. He could have simply said "Racing – backing horses – winning money" but even having padded it out slightly, he had to admit it was narrowly focused and one dimensional.

However, the Major's invisible switch had been flicked and he sat silent and content, sipping his gin and tonic and gazing wistfully about him while Baxter slipped away to the course betting shop and backed the first of his Epsom fancies. When that won, he left a bet on the other and returned to the Major who now looked animated and energetic once again.

"Ah, Baxter, in this next race Sir Michael Stoute of Newmarket has told me that Plumbed Oasis will win."

Baxter looked at the race card.

"But he doesn't train the horse" he argued.

The Major looked uncomfortable for a moment before recovering.

"That wasn't what I said. Anyway, I believe him."

With this he moved off to the same rails bookmaker as before. The man and his clerk were all smiles as he approached and it seemed they had a good relationship with him.

The connection between Sir Michael Stoute and Plumbed Oasis, who came from a tiny West Country stable, was obtuse but despite this it seemed to have a reasonable chance in an open handicap and Baxter had a hundred on it.

"Never got in the race!" said Baxter later as he disposed of his ticket in an exaggerated fashion of disgust.

"Bad jockey!" said the Major, who had no binoculars and who could hardly have seen the race. "Let's have another drink."

The Major insisted on buying the drinks once again and Baxter noticed he carried a purse and, each time, he would prise from its recesses a £10 note which had been folded into a small square.

"Don't worry, Baxter, I've got more information for later" the Major smiled.

Baxter's enthusiasm wasn't quite as evident as earlier and he received the news with neutrality. He was embroiling himself in the form for the next race when the Major spoke quietly.

"All these people pursuing life, trying to succeed, willing to enjoy the process. Fascinating isn't it?"

"Uhm," said Baxter, not anxious to engage in philosophy when he'd just dropped a century. "What's the tip here?" he said abruptly.

"The tip here – and once again the trainer phoned me personally – is Lancelot."

Baxter spluttered a mouthful of whisky across his face.

"That can't win, it's useless!" he muttered wiping his mouth and attending the damp spots on his clothes. "If the rest of the runners dropped dead it would still fall over their bodies."

"Well, I'm backing it" said the Major stubbornly.

"I can't believe you've had a tip for that" went on Baxter. "If that wins, I'll eat my hat. And yours too!" he shouted as the dumpy figure moved towards the ring.

A little later, the Major returned smiling.

"Big price, 20-1."

Baxter shook his head dismally.

"Should be 200-1 for what chance its got."

Baxter felt himself getting worked up over Lancelot and the fact that the Major had backed it in spite of what he'd told him. Even when the horse trailed in last, it didn't give him any satisfaction because there was no way the horse could have won.

"Thank you, Baxter. I cut my bet back to £200 on account of what you said. I think we should resume to the bar."

Baxter bought the round this time. Somehow the sight of the purse and the squirming around to get the money out embarrassed him.

The Major was in a mood of repose, quiet but seemingly happy in Baxter's company.

Baxter, though, had now given up all hope of profiting from the Major's information after the outrageous tip for Lancelot. Sitting next to him, Baxter observed something else that was slightly out of harmony with his original impression of the Major for he was not, in fact, well turned out. His shirt showed fraying around the collar and there were a couple of stains on the tie. Also the tweed jacket had buttons missing from the cuffs and, finally, his shoes needed re-heeling.

Of course, these observations were quickly forgotten when he discovered his other Epsom fancy had won. There was nothing quite like the feeling of a well-upholstered wallet decided Baxter as he returned towards the bar.

As he approached, the Major was waiting for him and thrust a warm bun wrapped in a serviette into his hand.

"I've bought you a beef burger. I've eaten mine - they're not bad." His switch had been flicked - the eyes bright and keen. "Operatic Snore, that's what I've heard for this race. What d'you think, Baxter?"

"Eighteen runners in a maiden fillies' – it's a pin job" declared Baxter. "Too hard for me" he admitted, quite satisfied with his afternoon's work.

"The trainer's an old friend – I think I can rely on him.

Nice of him to ring me, don't you think?"

With this he made a purposeful but amusing departure towards the ring.

Meanwhile, Baxter, who didn't like beef burgers, took an exploratory bite of something the texture of cardboard and remembered why – he then deposited the material in a litter-bin.

Operatic Snore was unplaced.

"Doesn't matter how good the information is if your luck's out. Good job you backed the first winner" said Baxter, trying to offer some consolation.

"You're right, Baxter, but it's not as reliable as it used to be. Now, Ryan Price, there was a man you could put your house on if he told you one. We landed some nice gambles together."

"I bet you did" smiled Baxter, recalling some of the great man's tilts at the ring. "He really knew how to give the bookie's a bloody nose."

"Indeed he did." The Major paused. "I've had a good time in your company, Baxter, but I'm going to leave now - want to miss the crowd."

"That's okay, I've had enough anyway."

There was just one thing the Major had to do and that was to say goodbye to his bookmaker.

"How did we finish up?" asked the Major.

"All square" replied the bookmaker smiling. "Same as last year."

"And every year that I've been coming here" said his clerk cheerfully.

"That's good. Well goodbye, gentlemen, I hope to see you next year."

It was all very civilised, thought Baxter, but a bit pointless.

"So you lost all the winnings from the first race?" asked Baxter as they made their way towards the exit.

"Yes" said the Major "it's easier that way – no accounting to do."

Baxter felt a little bemused by the remark when the Major turned to him with a glistening eye.

"Could you get me a taxi, Baxter?" he said quickly.

"A taxi?"

"Yes, I mustn't be back late."

Baxter waved a cab over towards them and the Major climbed in.

"Where to?" asked the driver.

The reply startled both the driver and Baxter who exchanged looks of alarm.

"To the asylum, of course!"

There was an uneasy silence until Baxter took out a £50 note and handed it to the driver.

"You heard the Major" he said.

NEVER MENTIONED

The dread of Baxter and all racing tipsters was the losing run. The thing was you never knew when it was about to start. Of course, it started with a loser but it could be thankfully short, frustratingly long or fatally enduring. Baxter's longest such run began the day after the Cheltenham Gold Cup, the winner of which he had not only tipped to his clients but had also backed and - dishonest as this may seem - the two didn't always go in tandem. He was feeling quite jaunty as he sat in his office for it also happened to be his birthday. Although it was much like any other day for him, he had in his mail at home received two birthday cards from his aunts and one from a distant cousin who he hadn't seen for a decade and whom he suspected was doing the basic groundwork for an inheritance. Had the relative made proper inquiries into Baxter's lifestyle and assets he would not have bothered.

However, the fact that he had tipped a big race winner was not only comforting but particularly useful in future advertising and guaranteed to bring in more clients. He looked up as his landlady approached the open door to his office.

"Good morning Mrs Wilbow – did you know I tipped the winner of the Cheltenham Gold Cup yesterday?"

"Oh, that is unusual" she replied.

Baxter wasn't sure whether she meant it was unusual to have tipped the Cheltenham Gold Cup winner or that he had tipped any winner at all. Whatever it was, it was not a compliment.

She pushed an envelope in front of him.

"Happy birthday, Mr Baxter."

"Well, thank you" said Baxter opening it.

"I tried to get one of those cards with your age on but I couldn't remember how old you were." Her cunning was very transparent.

"Never mind" replied Baxter who was rather sensitive about his age "I'm a year older than I was last year."

"Alright, don't tell me your age then but what about my rent, I know how much that is?"

Baxter took a rent book from his drawer, peeled off several notes from a wallet of considerable girth and passed them to Mrs Wilbow. She smiled and sighed apologetically as she took the money and entered it into the book. It turned out to be the last payment for a considerable time.

The losses in the following week were quite normal and extended to the second week but then success seemed at hand when his very best informant rang him from Newmarket. The man was shrewd and reliable and Baxter decided to have a thick bet on the animal himself. He travelled to Doncaster to watch it and all seemed well until halfway when suddenly the horse began to drop further and further back until it was losing more ground than an anorexic tug-of-war team. The animal finished last, just in time to avoid being involved in the next race.

The bad run continued - defeats by a sneeze, neck, half a length, it didn't matter – none of his selections could get their head in front. Subscribers began to stop phoning in, new subscribers slowed to a trickle and the premium tipping line was getting fewer calls than an octogenarian stripper. Baxter's confidence was shaken, soon he had surpassed his previous longest losing run – he was into unknown territory.

At the beginning of March, Baxter sent all his clients rejoinders to renew their subscription for the forthcoming flat season. The replies were scarce and not encouraging. Some had taken advantage of Baxter's stamped-addressed envelope to convey their opinions of the SureFire Tipping Service. Among the less offensive was one that had written across the subscription renewal form 'I WOULD RATHER POKE MYSELF IN THE EYE WITH A STICK'. Baxter considered this an extremely painful option and made a mental note to avoid any racegoer wearing an eye-patch. Despite this uncompromising message, Baxter still looked in the envelope for an accompanying cheque. Unfortunately, miracles were not on the agenda.

It was obvious to Baxter that new and better contacts were required – the trouble was they were as hard to find as a black cat in a darkened cellar. However, with this desperate need in mind he found himself agreeing to join a racing syndicate.

Toby Garrett had been a client of Baxter's for many years and when Toby rang him it was difficult to refuse. The horse was a 3-year-old colt named Grandad Fighting that had been brought over from Ireland to Newmarket. The disquieting news for Baxter was that the horse was to be trained by Ted Kinsella, a charming but unreliable Irishman.

"You're not serious! Not after what happened with Exploding Hair?"

What had happened with Exploding Hair was that the horse had been laid out for a handicap at Beverley. Kinsella, the trainer had inadvertently given it a strong workout the morning of the race thinking it was racing later that week. Not being told of this oversight, the conspirators had done their dough in style with Exploding Hair beaten a short head in a race it would surely have won. The truth only came out later when Kinsella announced he thought the horse was up to winning anyway! Baxter was seldom privy to conspiracies of the turf but had been up to his neck in this one and had good reason for his aversion to the Irishman.

"We all make mistakes" countered Toby. "In fact, most of your tips are!"

The laughter at the end of the phone mollified Baxter a little.

"Besides, Grandad Fighting is fit to run and Kinsella says he'll set him up for a race where we can go for a touch. And don't forget he's landed a few lately so he can do the business."

Baxter was won over and as Kinsella was a gambling stable it meant that he might hear of other stable plots he could profit from. So it was from this little ray of hope that Baxter took some comfort as he entered his office. A more substantial comfort was in the generous glass of Macallan he poured himself. The fiery liquid gave him instant warmth and was an added cloak not just from the reality of his loss of form but the consequences on his financial position. There were two letters for him. One was a charity appeal which he didn't even open and the other was his bank statement which he didn't want to open. It showed an account extensively overdrawn including a standing order to the racing syndicate. Baxter hoped Grandad Fighting would get a race soon as the last thing he needed was an expensive pet.

From his drawer, he pulled out the fact sheet that Kinsella had produced for the syndicate. The information was extensive. Bought for 12000 euros as a yearling, Grandad Fighting had run 3 times unplaced but with promise, acted on any going, had a preference to go left-handed and was bred to stay. The horse's bloodline was shown together with the details of all his races to date. Although the picture at the top of the page indicated the colt was no world-beater, all Baxter required of the plain-looking animal was a good thrashing of a few bookmakers.

It was more than a week later that Toby finally rang Baxter to confirm that Grandad Fighting was entered to run at York. According to the trainer, the horse was ready and sure to run a big race and Toby was taking the day off to go.

The race was on a Friday and Baxter met Tony and several of the other syndicate members at York station. The whole lot of them got into Tony's people carrier and drove to the course. The weather had been very good of late and Baxter discovered that the course had been watered. He discussed this with Toby who didn't think it made any difference as Grandad Fighting was reported to go on any ground. They also learned that although the horse had arrived safely at the course, the trainer hadn't and was therefore unable to reassure its keen owners that the horse should be backed and to what extent.

It was shortly before the start of the first race that dramatically and suddenly, brooding grey clouds appeared and bulldozed their way into the sky above the Knavesmire. The rain fell with an intensity that had it bouncing off the ground and the horses and jockeys returned from the first race looking like they'd passed under a waterfall.

Fortunately, by the time Grandad Fighting was due to run the rain had ceased, the sun had returned and the syndicate members were able to attend the parade ring in reasonable comfort. There was no doubt though that the rain had got into the ground and Baxter noted that it was becoming a ploughed field on the inside of the track and in such conditions he wasn't keen to have any sort of bet.

As they watched their horse parading, there was a chirrup from Toby's mobile phone.

"A little bit of hush everyone, it's our trainer!" he appealed.

After a couple of minutes, Toby relayed the information to everyone.

"Mr Kinsella has been delayed. Apparently, he broke down on the motorway but he should be here quite soon."

"I thought he'd just bought a new car – should have been reliable" said a voice.

"Yes, but not without petrol" said Toby wryly. "Anyway, the good news is that Grandad Fighting will not be inconvenienced by the change in the going, he will run a big race and we are recommended to back it."

There was a chorus of approval – optimism was in the air and Baxter was reconsidering. What was decisive in his decision to have a crack on Grandad Fighting was the conversation with the jockey. He was one of the older jockeys riding and while his riding technique was modest he used his experience to compensate. What he told the assembled owners was that there was a fast track of ground on the outside of the course because only the inside two thirds had been watered. Having ridden in the earlier races he reckoned that if Grandad Fighting could race on the wide outside and then cut back in on the turn for home he could have a big enough lead to hold on and steal it. Toby, Baxter and the rest were enthusiastic about the plan as there was nothing to their knowledge to suggest it wouldn't work. So it was all agreed and the syndicate members dispersed with some confidence to give a good hiding or at least a slap to their selected bookmaker.

Because of his reservations regarding Kinsella, Baxter had resisted putting Grandad Fighting on his tipping line but he was completely won over by the idea of taking advantage of the better ground on the outside of the course. Eights was the general price about the colt as he scouted around the joints. Quite soon that disappeared and sevens was the general call and Baxter was annoyed with himself for not getting on immediately knowing the syndicate money was almost bound to shorten the price.

He made a quick dart to his left, where a bit of 15 to 2 was available, when his left ankle suddenly gave way and he found himself bathing in one of the numerous puddles that were around. A searing jolt of pain came from his foot and, as some helpful arms lifted him up, any thoughts of his bet had disappeared. Baxter couldn't stand on the injured foot and sat unhappily on the bottom steps of the terracing.

With a grimacing face, all Baxter's focus was in the pain pulsing out from his foot, which he decided must be broken. Someone must have notified a man from St John's who was now kneeling down and starting to undo Baxter's

"Sat unhappily on the bottom steps of the terracing"

shoe. He prodded the foot around and asked Baxter to move his toes. The sock had also been removed and Baxter could see his ankle resembled the mound at Stratford.

"You've not broken it" said the first-aid man. "Just a severe sprain, which I'm going to strap up for you."

Once the heavy bandage had been applied, Baxter felt considerably better. On went the sock but the shoe had to be left undone. Baxter stood up and when the man let go of him, he found he could stand even if it was with considerable pain.

Then from a murmur, there erupted a roar of noise from the crowd around him. The race was under way and the horses were turning into the straight! From the giant TV screen he could see the black and red colours of the syndicate with a good lead and he remembered he wasn't on! What stinking luck – done his foot in and missed a winner! And then suddenly Grandad Fighting seemed to be going up and down in the same spot and a wall of horses gobbled him up like he had a 'PLEASE PASS' sign on the back of his silks.

Baxter dragged the injured foot and limped back towards the unsaddling enclosure. No one seemed to notice Baxter's incapacity as he rejoined Toby and the others.

There was disappointment amongst them but nothing more. These were racing people and this was how the game went sometimes. They were in it for the sport unlike Baxter who was also in it for a living.

"Well beaten" was Toby's verdict. "The jockey did everything right. I thought we'd win on the turn for home. I'm not sure what went wrong."

Baxter was silent. He still didn't feel too good but

listened to the earnest debate amongst the others, which was suddenly interrupted by an Irish voice.

"I understand Grandad Fighting didn't win so I hope you didn't lose too much money."

Kinsella had arrived smiling and was greeting his owners.

"I'm sorry I missed the race so tell me exactly how it went?" he asked Toby.

Toby explained the race tactics that failed and Kinsella listened carefully. "Well, racing alone on the far side on the better ground and then switching to the rails on the home turn were excellent tactics but for one glaring mistake."

"Which was?" asked Toby.

"Well, I thought I put it down on the horse's fact sheet but then again it's possible I never mentioned it. The truth is that Grandad Fighting has to be covered up - absolutely essential!"

It was clear from the expression on the faces around him that he had indeed omitted this important information.

"Oh dear" he added.

Kinsella had done it again thought Baxter but this time it hadn't caused him any damage. Of course, he'd hurt his foot but he still reckoned his luck had just changed.

Visit the website: www.baxterstories.co.uk

RACING STORIES
by
ROY GRANVILLE

If you enjoyed this book, you may like to know that the first Baxter Vs. The Bookies is available in its Second Edition from bookshops or direct from:

HAYES PRESS
P.O. BOX 489
HAYES
UB3 2WZ

Tel: 0208 561 3133

Price £9.95 (postage & package free)